He covered her hand with his own

"Christina, I know that whatever is worrying you seems as large as a mountain, but I really can help." Ashley gave her a smile of encouragement. "Money may not solve all problems, but it can help, and influence can help a great deal more."

She considered his offer, then shook her head. "It might not be as bad as I thought, I mean I haven't seen . . ." She couldn't tell him she hadn't seen the headlines that would certainly have filled the newspapers if what she feared most had eventuated. She couldn't tell him—not yet, at least.

"Please," she entreated, "let's not think of it now. I'd just like to enjoy tonight. It's so lovely here."

Unexpectedly, the hand over hers departed, and Ashley raised his glass with purpose. "To a closer acquaintance, then."

Mons Daveson remembers sending off her first manuscript after a great deal of work—only to have it rejected. She is now, however, a seasoned author who appreciates the pleasures and frustrations that come with writing. "There is a certain feeling you get when you start a story," she explains, "a story that has been building, little by little, segment by segment, within the mind, and see the actual words written down." It is a feeling of satisfaction once all the sentences and paragraphs finally come together. Mons grew up in the ruggedly beautiful Australian outback, has visited all parts of her country and now lives with her family in Brisbane.

Books by Mons Daveson

HARLEQUIN ROMANCE
2461—LAND OF TOMORROW
2534—MY LORD KASSEEM
2575—MACKENZIE COUNTRY
2756—GIRL OF MYSTERY

These books may be available at your local bookseller.

Don't miss any of our special offers. Write to us at the following address for information on our newest releases.

Harlequin Reader Service
901 Fuhrmann Blvd.
P.O. Box 1325, Buffalo, NY 14269
Canadian address: P.O. Box 2800, Postal Station A,
5170 Yonge St., Willowdale, Ont. M2N 6J3

Girl of Mystery

Mons Daveson

Harlequin Books

TORONTO • NEW YORK • LONDON
AMSTERDAM • PARIS • SYDNEY • HAMBURG
STOCKHOLM • ATHENS • TOKYO • MILAN

Original hardcover edition published in 1984
by Mills & Boon Limited

ISBN 0-373-02756-7

Harlequin Romance first edition April 1986

Printed in U.S.A.

CHAPTER ONE

THE crash of metal smashing into the kerb as the heavy car was swung sideways; the screech of brakes too hastily, too abruptly, applied; the sound of superbly engineered machinery trying to obey instructions sent to it by brain and hands, echoed loudly. It was all too late—by the fraction of a second. There came the noise of a ton of metal and upholstery meeting softness. . . .

Beneath the blazing headlights which had been left on full strength, unable to make herself move, she was yet still aware of the driver of this juggernaut rounding the bonnet with a rush; of him bending over; of his hands reaching down, not trying to move her, just feeling. She also heard the blistering sentence directed at himself.

Vaguely, through the mists of shock from the thud with which she had been hit—though not nearly as heavily as it would have been if the car hadn't been so expertly handled—she realised he was blaming himself . . . and it hadn't been his fault.

She had been looking the other way for traffic, and as it was clear, had moved on to the road—no, not the road; into the busy highway that this was—the main thoroughfare into Surfers Paradise.

'Be still!' barked the man who was only an outline looming above; only an immaculate trousered leg kneeling in the dirt beside her. A tone slurred, probably also from shock at what had occurred, went through the dazed mind of the girl, trying even now to move. She also tried ineffectually to thrust away those exploring hands, trying to rise on an elbow.

At her movement, and further, at the murmur coming from her, for a murmur was all she could manage, she heard a voice saying with what sounded

5

like thankfulness, 'It's a child, and it's alive, thank the lord!' as he seemed to take in the big eyes gazing up at him from the blur of a pale face half hidden by fair shining hair.

His words came distinct enough for her to hear, and she replied, 'I'm not a child, and I'm all right,' as she again began to push away his roving hands with such a gesture of repudiation that the man abruptly drew back.

'I'm all right,' the words were repeated, and the voice came clipped and assured, even if sounding somewhat shaky as she endeavoured to move upright.

Helped by hard impersonal fingers, she leant back against the fender of the long grey car. The girl looked at him, this man whose car had knocked her down, and as she tried to straighten, winced.

'Look, I'll get you to a doctor, unless. . . .' she heard the hesitation as if he was unwilling to complete the sentence, and then the curt authoritative finish of it, 'you want to report the accident to the police.'

'No!' The exclamation interrupted him so sharply, that the eyes of the man before her narrowed, and he looked her over more thoroughly. She straightened as much as she was able, using every inch of her slender average height, an assurance that would once have been a normal attribute, but which had now deteriorated, to return that glance.

Receiving it, he spoke. 'You're young, much too young, to be out at night by yourself. Especially in this resort town, where anything goes. You should be home, tucked up in bed long since by your mother. And why the "No" in that tone?' The slur had left the voice, sending it crisp, authoritative. 'If you don't want it reported to the police, you're still going to a doctor. I don't want anything backfiring at me, thank you very much.'

'I tell you, I'm quite all right. You can go now. Thank you for stopping and helping me up.' Dismissal was implicit in her words.

'I'm afraid, however, you'll have to allow me to tell *you*, my dear child,' steel had come to override the curious slur that seemed the normal tone in which he spoke, 'that I am not going. I'm either driving you to a doctor, or taking you home. Do you live here in Surfers or on the Gold Coast . . .?' He broke off. One lone car which had been cruising along stopped alongside, a driver looking curiously out of his window at them.

'What's going on here? Are you in trouble?' He was looking the long opulent Jaguar over, but his glance was more interested in the young girl.

Whether she heard the angry expletive which issued from the man's lips or not, he didn't know, but it was she who turned to say calmly:

'No, there's no trouble. I ran out into the road after a kitten I thought was going to get run over, and I'm just being told off for it.' The words were said oh, so carelessly, with a smiling face, but the girl still leaned against the metal fender behind her.

Both men looked at one another, then both shrugged, their thoughts showing in that action. A half-wave came from a car window, an engine purred, and a car departed.

She might not have been able to see it in the uncertain light, but the eyebrows belonging to the figure beside her climbed. 'That was a very clever story, thought out as it must have been at a split second's notice. Does that fact denote acting ability, or a very great need for no publicity? Because if it's the latter, it won't work with me. I'm either taking you home, right to your door, or to a doctor. Now, take your pick.' His tone brooked no argument.

As she pushed herself away from the car's fender, the wince as she did so was unmistakable, but her words were just as firm as his had been. 'I don't live here. I *am* all right, and, I am *not* going to a doctor. I'm going to a bus depot on my way to Brisbane.'

'At this time of night?' A hand went up, a watch was

looked at. 'At almost one o'clock in the morning?'
Disbelief coloured the words. Then as she was turning
deliberately away, he saw her leg in the faint light and
with a startled exclamation swung her round to stand
before the blazing headlights.

Blood was oozing copiously from a badly grazed leg,
seeping right down and over the instep. He said no
more, but the girl found herself swept up and dropped
in the front seat of the car, the man crowding in beside
her.

'It won't open, it's locked,' his voice said, as her
fingers went out to fumble at the catch, and the tone
carried no amusement whatever. 'So you'd just better
sit still and we'll go to my home, as you don't appear to
have one. I'll have you checked over, then we'll see
what has to be done.'

Quietly the big car moved forward, along the
highway, into and past the heart of Surfers Paradise. It
was still blazing with neon, but had not the frenzied
brightness that an earlier hour would have shown. The
driver swung the wheel and the vehicle turned towards
the Esplanade and the ocean. Suddenly, so abruptly as
to make itself felt, the noise and the brightness of the
famous tourist resort town had disappeared. They had
passed far below the ground into an underground car
park. The Jaguar purred into what was apparently its
reserved garage, a seat-belt was unsnicked and with a
fluidity that betokened perfect physical co-ordination,
the man had twisted out of his seat.

He must have touched a switch or pressed a button
on the dashboard, because when he touched the
passenger seat handle it slid open at once. He put out a
hand to help her, but stood back sharply as she shrank
away, descending by herself.

'I'm known here, I don't want any disturbance,' a
cold voice said. 'Are you coming up to my place
quietly or do I call the police to take you off my
hands?' An arm went out in a throw-away gesture

towards a phone hanging on the wall between some elevators.

No answer being forthcoming, he moved towards them, the slight figure following after. He didn't press for the lift either. He searched among the keys on a ring he carried, and apparently finding what he wanted, inserted one in a plaque set there and turned.

The lift door before them slid open, and the small enclosed space carried only silence as it shot upwards. It was a luxuriously enclosed space, however. Deep carpet into which the feet sank covered the floor. Embossed panelled walls, upon one a mirror, positioned high enough to check one's face in. Opposite it, a pastel watercolour of Surfers Paradise beach showed it on a sundrenched day. Neither of the passengers looked into the mirror.

When they stepped from the lift, it wasn't into a foyer on to which any number of units opened. It, too, like the lift, was thickly carpeted, with only a solitary door facing them. Again, a key was inserted, and stepping back, the man indicated that she should walk through. Because she had to, she obeyed—into a huge living room from another world—an Eastern world.

She was given no time to look about her. The bunch of keys was thrown on to a table beside the entrance, a jacket which had been carried from the car carelessly hooked over a shoulder was tossed on to a lounge seat, glinting as the satin lining hung open anyhow. The man turned to his reluctant guest.

'Well now,' he said. 'My name is Ashley Carlton. I think it's time I knew yours also. What is it?' That curious slur had returned to his tone again, as if now relaxed, he was speaking naturally.

As no answer was forthcoming, an eyebrow rose, and he moved to a phone on a side table.

'I forget! I must have hit my head when the car knocked me down.' Baldly the sentence came.

If it could have been said to go higher, the man's

right eyebrow did. So also did the furious expletive as it issued from his lips. She knew from the sound of it that it was an oath, but she didn't know what it meant. It had emerged violently in another language.

'Look, I've had enough of this.' These words were uttered in English, tightly from between compressed lips. So was his touch tight when he caught hold of her shoulder. Even he, in his anger, saw a wince that wasn't faked.

'You're hurt, aren't you?'

As she still remained silent, he swung away to the table holding the phone. 'I'll get my doctor first, and then the police. They'll have to be notified if you're hurt. But I've had enough! I've had a bloody night all through, and I want to put it away into yesterday.'

'Please . . . please don't. . . .'

Fingers stopped after dialling three digits and he turned to look at her . . . and taking note of the expression in her eyes, he returned the phone to its cradle.

'Please don't call a doctor,' the repeated words came. 'I really wasn't hurt. My shoulder and arm were caught and are probably bruised a little, and my leg is grazed, but that's all.'

They both looked down at her leg, still slowly oozing blood. And it was the girl who said, 'I don't want to get it on the carpet.'

On hearing such a mundane remark, the man called Ashley laughed, sounding normal for the first time. He moved suddenly, scooping the slight figure into his arms—and wasn't prepared for the violent effort she made to get free, or the look of fright that overwhelmed the pale face.

'I'm only carrying you to the bathroom—and I might add,' he continued as he pushed open a door in a corridor opening off the huge living room, 'that rape is the last thought in my mind at the present moment. And that also, even if it was, I think I might want someone a little more attractive than you appear just now, however you might look when dressed properly and in your right mind.'

Brought out of a nightmare that had seemed to enfold her for more hours than she cared to remember by those blistering words, the girl gave a quick surreptitious glance at the full-length mirror. She saw fair hair, normally smooth and shining as it curved round her cheeks to lie on her shoulders, but that was now tangled in what one used to call rats' tails, salt-saturated from not being washed after her swim this afternoon. A face having no colour at all except for a long smear of blood that must have been carried from her leg by a careless hand: large eyes which still held strain and, yes, further back, fright. In the bright overhead light they showed amber with what seemed flecks of green. Eyebrows only a shade darker than her hair stretched up and outwards.

Behind the frightened look, behind all the strain, came anger that he had spoken so brusquely, and so disparagingly, about her. Then at her back his figure showed reflected, and the astringent smell of disinfectant flowed about them.

'Come along, I'll bathe that leg.' White teeth smiled in the tanned face behind her, but she turned from that smile, shying away.

'I can manage now,' she told him, standing against the wall behind her.

'Don't be so stupid! Get that sandal off.' A hand reached down to remove it from the blood-stained foot. He found it in his hand, but its owner had moved further from him.

The expression on the tanned face changed from pleasantness to a deep scowl, the eyes, dark blue, taking on bleakness. The whole countenance turned suddenly from open friendliness to a cold, chill ruthlessness. But before he could put into practice the intention she saw so plainly in that determined, angry face, a soft voice broke in on them—speaking in a language she couldn't understand.

The girl turned, arms outstretched, so obviously at bay that the two men stood back, unmoving. Then it was the man who had called himself Ashley Carlton who spoke, and also in that unintelligible language. There appeared no hesitation, no searching for a word or nuance. The sentences flowed back and forth between the two men, one so obviously Chinese or of that ethnic background, the other so Nordic; so Australian or English. Skin a dark brown, certainly, but only from a life in the sun of this climate. Blue eyes, darker than she had first thought, coloured as they were with a blaze of anger, and hair that was fairer than her own, which resembled the dull yellow of gold, while his showed more the shade of lemon, of citrine, and in places was streaked to almost platinum.

Now both his hands flew up in a gesture of irritation, and he stood back, the sandal still held. He glanced at it without seeming to take it in, then his glance focused, and an ironic smile parted his lips. He glanced from it to the other sandal still on her foot, then assessed her whole figure. She didn't understand that look, and without knowing why, felt a flush burn her cheeks.

Well, she wasn't a pauper, this unknown waif he had knocked down, thought the man in the bathroom doorway. He had paid for enough feminine clothes and fripperies in the last dozen years to know definitely that these sandals and that dress didn't come from a chain-store rack. They had imported exclusiveness patterned all over them.

'Will you allow me to see to your hurt, miss? I do have some training to do so. I acted as a para-medic among the people in my own country.' The voice was soft, the English only faintly accented.

The girl pressed back against the wall, looked at him, but couldn't read the expression on that unfamiliar face. Still, the tone sounded kind, so she nodded—and the owner of the place shrugged carelessly, turned his back and departed.

'Sit on that chair, and put your foot on my knee ... so,' the soft Chinese voice said. He had pulled forward a fragile vanity chair for her, and sat on the edge of the bathtub with a folded towel across one knee. Carefully, gently, he bathed off the blood and gravel; the cotton wool balls dipped into the warm milk-white liquid, pristine fresh, then discarded stained pink. 'There, that will do, I think.' The bent-over head came up and smiled at her. 'You will find it is not too bad; a nasty scab for some days, but no scarring ... expecially no scarring after I put ointment on it. Just wait! I'll get it.'

The girl's gaze went up to what seemed a well-stocked cabinet on the wall, but the para-medic's head shook from side to side. 'No, I have better from my own country. Please just wait.'

She waited and looked about her—at the shining luxurious bathroom, tiles gleaming, chrome glittering from the reflection of overhead lights, to through the doorway of a bedroom from which this room opened off, then down to her leg. It had been washed clean and showed glinting red in places where the skin had been rubbed off, although a large part of the calf didn't, as the man said, look too bad. Then her so-called para-medic was back and raising her leg again to his knee, spread the wound liberally with a dark-coloured ointment. Her nose wrinkled at the smell that floated upwards towards her.

'Yes, it is not a pleasant aroma, is it?' said the Chinese man, 'but you will find it is very satisfactory. There. . . .' gauze had been lightly placed, a bandage passed round and tied, and he stood up. 'You are to sleep in here, miss, Mr Ashley says.' He collected the used medicaments and discarded impedimenta, and as softly and silently as he seemed to do everything, he left.

Standing in the middle of the bedroom, the girl

looked about her. This was no Eastern room, though it was beautiful and as luxurious as was the one she had just left, it was just a run-of-the-mill Australian bedroom. Pale green carpet, curtains to match, cream-frilled bedspread, with upon it the same pale green-coloured satin comforter doubled upon its foot. She took it all in, then went to the door and turned the little catch within the knob, locking it.

Back she went to the bathroom and rummaged among bottles and jars in that cabinet, words sounding in her memory. 'And if I did I would want someone more attractive than you appear'. She knew she didn't want any man's attention ... any man's. But she did want to look presentable.

Running water into the basin, she reached down a container of shampoo, lathering her hair quickly. It wasn't dirty, only salt-saturated from the ocean. Rinsing it swiftly with clean water, she rubbed it briskly over and over. Almost dry, she took up her handbag from where it had been dropped and extracted a comb, combing it into place, patting it under to lie like some mediaeval pageboy bob sloping from her eyes down past her cheeks to lie on her shoulders. Ruefully, she gazed at the other articles which the bag contained. Compact and lipstick, tissues, a small change purse. She opened it. A one-dollar note and some silver met her gaze. Suddenly, the strain and fright were back in the amber-green eyes and she walked over to the chair before the dressing-table and dropped into it. What was she to do—and more to the point, what had she left behind? She shuddered, the ripple going through her whole body. What if. . . .

A soft knock upon the door jerked her upright, and raising a frightened face from hands that had covered it, she looked fearfully in that direction. The knock came again.

'Yes?' she called, making no attempt to open it.

'It is Han, miss. I have brought you some Ovaltine.'

She came upright, a little unsteadily, and moved across to turn the little knob. He stood there with a tray in one hand on which reposed a tall glass of chocolate-coloured liquid. His other hand carried some folded garments.

'It's a pair of Mr Ashley's pyjamas for you, miss. They are new and have not been worn. And drink this up, it will help you sleep.' He walked past her, placing the glass on the bedside table, and, folding back the quilt over the eiderdown at the bottom of the bed, set the pyjamas on a pillow. 'Goodnight, miss,' he said then, and left.

Her glance following him, she gazed at the closed door and suddenly knew she had no need to follow and lock it. She pulled off her dress that, even after all the wear and tear to which it had been subjected, still looked what it was—an expensive original. Under it was not bra and pants, but a bikini. These too she discarded, and picked up the pyjama top. No silk was this, but thin, fine cotton, maroon with a narrow white binding. Fastening the buttons, she glanced across the room into the mirror. She really had no need to don the bottoms, the top came right past her thighs almost to her knees. She rolled up the sleeves.

Switching off the overhead light, she climbed into bed, pulling up the light covering to her chin. As she turned to extinguish the bed-lamp her gaze alighted on the glass. She hadn't eaten since lunch long hours ago, and it was now—she looked at her watch, slim-lined, gold, set in a fragile-seeming band: almost two o'clock. Gingerly she sipped, and finding the liquid carried the familiar taste of Ovaltine, drank it all. Flipping out the light, she settled down, knowing she wouldn't sleep ... knowing the horrendous happenings of the evening would not let her. Her arm dropped from across her face on to the turned-down sheet, her eyelids drooped, and she didn't know she had fallen into sleep almost at once; she didn't know, either, that her drink had had a supplement. And she wasn't aware of the conversation going on in a much larger bedroom than the one she occupied, of which she was the burning subject.

CHAPTER TWO

THE room about her was dim, and yet still had the clearness of day. Eyes opening slowly, she gazed round it, puzzled, wondering at the strangeness. Then abruptly came recollection and the girl sat up swiftly with a glance at her wrist watch. It was just after nine o'clock. A frown came between the finely etched brows. Her sleep had been deep, unbroken, she realised. She had not stirred from when she had slipped down under the covers until now. Her glance rested on the used glass, and acknowledgment came. They, or at least, Han, had laced it with some sort of sleeping medication.

Slipping out of bed, she padded on bare feet to the window. Only the touch of a button by the curtain was necessary to send the curtains swinging wide.

'Oh . . . ooh . . .!' The gasp came involuntarily. The view was breathtaking. These windows here didn't look straight out on to the ocean front, but obliquely sideways, facing the north. A few high-rise buildings, reaching to the sky, etched themselves against vivid blueness, but as far as the eye could see was the ocean, restless, ever-moving, white-capped as it broke upon silver sands, dazzling the gaze with the brilliance of its blue-green rushing breakers.

For a few seconds more she stood there, then her eyes regained their hint of strain, of frightened conjecture, and she turned determinedly and moved to the bathroom. She bathed, if awkwardly in the tub, endeavouring not to wet the bandage, and found that her leg hardly hurt at all this morning. She dressed in the only clothes she possessed, then, lipsticked and combed, she drew a deep steadying breath and, walking to the door, opened it.

In the short corridor outside, a door faced her own, and at its end on an otherwise blank wall was also a door. Probably a suite like the one she had just come from opposite—the other, most likely, extending the length of the unit, would no doubt be the master bedroom. . . . She turned abruptly and stepped into the huge living-room.

Last night she had only gained an impression. Now, in the brightness of broad day, she gazed in delight— even with a carefully guarded delight. It was into an Eastern atmosphere that she went. Golden paper, not bright gold, but muted, coloured the walls. Superimposed sparsely on or within it were etched, in brilliant turquoise and emerald, the strangest birds and plants she had ever seen. The carpet was also coloured the same muted gold, thick and soft to cushion sound.

The faces of two old Chinese peasants, one male, one female, jumped out to catch the eye, so painted that they seemed almost alive as they looked for ever out at the beautiful room with its carved and mother-of-pearl inlaid furniture, its sofas and chairs with the curved lions' legs.

Finally, gazing beyond, the girl saw the wide glass doors opening on to a balcony, and glint of blue that was the ocean far in the distance. She walked down past an archway which a glance beyond showed was a formal dining-room, also from the East.

Another arch further along gave her pause. This was from no Far Eastern country, but right out of the newest American Home Beautiful, it came. Gleaming tiles on floor and walls, the glint of labour-saving gadgets everywhere, and facing her, smiling, was Han.

'Good morning, miss. Your breakfast is ready. Do you take tea or coffee?' He gestured, and she saw a small table set for one in an alcove separated from the kitchen proper by shelves filled with glassware.

She hesitated, wanting to ask questions, yet not wanting to be involved. She did say, 'Yes, thank you,'

and went to the chair he was holding for her. As he put
a plate piled with scrambled eggs before her, she said
again, 'Thank you. Will you please tell me what to call
you?'

'My name is Han, miss. There is a lot more also, but
Mr Ashley just calls me Han. Is there a name by which
I can call you?'

It was said softly, expectantly, but the girl's head
went down and she dropped back the fork she had
picked up.

'Very well, maybe later perhaps. Eat your breakfast
now.' The words were said in the tone of voice of an
adult humouring a child, and a stain of pink rose to
colour the down-bent face. Unhappily she took up the
fork again and began to eat, finding unexpectedly that
she was ravenous. As a cup and saucer were set down
by her plate, she glanced at her servitor and said shyly,
'Did you put a sleeping tablet in my Ovaltine last night,
Han?'

'Oh no, miss, not a sleeping tablet, but I did put some
herbs in—that come from my country. I thought you
needed to sleep.'

'Yes, I did . . . thank you. Now, can I say thank you
again for your kindness and the breakfast, and will you
please show me the way out.'

'Sorry! You're not to go, Mr Ashley said. He will be
back before lunch and will talk to you then.'

'But of course I'm going . . . now!' she told him
angrily as he stood there so calmly smiling.

'Where are you going, miss? Home? Then Mr Ashley
will take you.'

'Where I'm going is my business. And I'm leaving
now!' The girl picked up the small beach-bag which she
had carried from the bedroom and slung it over her
shoulder, then turned to move towards the archway.

'The entrance door is locked, miss—with a deadlock
which has to be opened with a key from the inside as
well as from the outside. Look, there are the Sunday

papers, read them out on the balcony until Mr Ashley comes home.'

'I don't want to read the papers, and I *am* going. This is ridiculous! You can't hold me here. You'll have me thinking I've run into some kind of a racket! And,' she gestured widely round the beautiful unfamiliar living-room, 'from the looks of this place, it could well belong to that sort of thing.' Frustration made the voice run high.

The bland Chinese face smiled, but it spoke gently. 'There is no need for you to worry. This is Mr Ashley's home. This,' in his turn he gestured to the Eastern setting, 'comes from Vietnam where he served in that war. It reminds him of a time, and a person, he was happy with. Please, just to wait, he will be here soon.'

Unwillingly, she stood. But what else could she do . . . and then she thought of something she *could* do, so, shrugging, she picked up the papers and moved out on to the balcony. She didn't begin reading the stories in the headlines, but scanned through all the pages, apparently searching for a particular item. In her concentration she did not realise that her actions were being watched as she turned page after page.

One large Sunday paper finished, she turned to the other one, and this she surveyed more closely. It too, as she reached the back pages, she laid aside. But the shadowed eyes still held their shadows. . . .

She sat gazing out over the sparkling ocean, at the people who seemed so tiny so far below, at the cars rushing head-tilt to their rendezvous, at the sun-worshippers on the silver sands, seeing none of it, a small, huddled figure, squeezed into a corner by the window.

She didn't hear the front door open, or notice the two men who entered at the far end of the big room. It was the voices that brought them to her attention.

'It's just as well I caught you on your way in, Ashley.' The words were uttered sharply. 'It's the stupidest thing

I know of, being unable to get up here in an elevator because your private one has to be serviced with a key ... and that dashed telephone recorder! You do it deliberately, so that you can't be reached.'

'But, Edmond,' the voice of her rescuer of last night held only amusement, 'I always return your phone calls, surely.'

'You return them ... in your own good time. And if you want to. I wonder what your friends think of never being able to reach you. I expect that's why there are so many calls for you at the office.'

'But, my dear Edmond, I have a secretary there who's just as efficient as my recorder. She sorts out all my calls and leaves messages just as it does, and she knows better than to put through anything but business calls. Now, tell me what's upset you this time. You do know,' here the tone in that voice changed, amusement departing, 'that I simply can't be bothered sometimes. I return all the calls I need to.'

'Yes, well, my boy,' this tone also had changed, the exasperation gone, 'I understand, but your aunt worries a bit. And you are booked with us for tonight, you know. She hasn't heard from you.'

'I'm sorry, I did forget. I've had more than a few things on my mind. Still, there's one thing you'll be pleased to know about, I expect,' amusement had crept into the tone again, 'and that is that you won't have to worry about what you call my extravagances so much now—for a while anyhow! I do sometimes feel like a small boy wasting his pocket money when you feel it's time to give me one of your lectures.'

'What do you mean? I've seen no signs of you cutting down your spending.'

'Well, no, but then I don't need to, do I? But I've just parted company with a cause of some of the extravagance you're always on about. It may have been unexpected, but it ended with a bang last night.'

'Not ...?'

'Oh yes. So you see my recorder comes in handy. No one can get at me at all up here.'

'Are you pleased, Ashley?' Sympathy clouded the older man's voice, and there was compassion too. 'She was very beautiful.'

'Oh, indeed she was . . . very! And very accommodating too. I thought, too, that she always gave value for any lavish expenditure showered upon her. Still, that's all water under the bridge now.'

'You wouldn't have thought of marriage, my boy. You know, it's time you really did settle down, start a family. I saw you both at that charity affair and thought what a magnificent couple you made.'

'Marriage, with Delice? Good God, no! That's the last thing! But it suited me while it lasted.' What was the nuance that that tone carried now? thought the listening girl. Acceptance . . . uninterest . . . she couldn't place it.

'Well then,' briskly the subject was changed, 'I was going to tell you tomorrow, but you might as well know now. There's a bit of upset out at the timber mill, both in the yard and in the office. Fenton's secretary is leaving. That doesn't matter, the other girl can move up a place, and we'll get a junior. It's the yard trouble I'm concerned about. We're inundated with orders, as you know. This affair will have to be cleared up right away.'

'All right, I'll get out there some time tomorrow, but Fenton is reliable: he can handle whatever it is. Also, I have quite a lot of work piling up on my desk at head office. Still, I'll go.'

Only silence echoed out to the balcony for a brief moment, and through the small slit of vision that was all she had, the girl could not see that Han was trying desperately to catch his master's attention.

'Yes, Fenton's a good chap. Nevertheless, you get out there. Now I'd better be off. We'll see you tonight at the barbecue, won't we? And Ashley, how about giving some thought to settling down? All right, all right!'

Edmond finished quickly as a sharp impatient sentence answered, but his nephew was adding, 'You'll have a drink, Edmond, before you go? Or perhaps stay to lunch?'

Han's hand went out in so apparent a gesture of rejection, but he needn't have worried. 'No, I won't stay, but yes, I will have a Scotch and water, please, Han.' Then with the amber-filled glass in his hand, he turned to the balcony.

.'There's one thing I'll give you about your eyrie up here, my boy,' he was saying as he walked through, 'even if I do abominate your telephone thingammybob, and that's your view.'

He was through the doorway, his glass to his mouth, drinking, when his gaze came to rest on the girl sitting hunched up in her corner. He choked, the Scotch going down the wrong way. He bent over, coughing violently. Rising, she stood silent, aware all the time of the quick-fire conversation going on behind their two selves in staccato Chinese or Vietnamese, or whatever the damn language was, she thought irritably.

'Who are you?' Finally the coughing had stopped and she found she was being subjected to an incredulous stare.

She didn't have to answer, however. A hand came out from behind the questioning figure and caught hold of one of hers lying limply down by her side, drew her inside. The form of the elderly man turned as if on a pivot as she passed him, still staring.

'Who is she, Ashley? you never have females up here . . . you never have anyone up here.'

'The point is, Edmond, I simply don't know how to tell you who she is. My little mystery girl tells me she's forgotten her name—since I ran over her last night with the Jaguar!'

He's enjoying this, thought the girl, trying to free her hand from that other hand's grasp, and not succeeding. In fact, his entire manner was different from what it had been last night. He was looking straight at his uncle with those dark blue eyes glinting amusement.

'Since you ran over her?' She thought their visitor was going to have apoplexy.

'Yes, last night.'

'But what's she doing here? Why isn't she in her own home? Have you been in touch with Sedgwick?'

It was the man called Ashley whose voice went high with surprise now. 'Oh, no, Uncle Edmond,' he said gently, 'I'm sure my little Miss Mystery wouldn't want me to get in touch with my lawyer. There's no need for it, is there, my unknown?' He was swinging the hand he held as if they were sauntering along on some picnic. Again she tried to free it, and again the grip tightened. 'She doesn't appear to want a doctor, or the police—so I can't imagine that a lawyer would be necessary.'

'But you could be ... it could be ... In your position, with your wealth. . . .'

'Surely, my dear uncle, you don't think it was a set-up? There was no way in the world it could have been. No one knew I was coming home from Brisbane; no one knew I would get bored with that celebration party. Winning the race was what mattered, and as the celebrations got wilder I found I'd had enough.' There was that curious nuance in his tone again, went through her mind as it had done out on the balcony, but he was continuing. 'And from there I went to Alicia's, where normally I would have stayed. I didn't. No, the accident was purely an accident.'

'What's your name, child?' The older man had turned back to her. Upright, elderly, silver-haired, but not a bit like the younger man standing beside him.

What should she say, or do? Should she just say she wanted to leave? Then she felt that grip tighten again, and knew she wouldn't be allowed to unless she gave some sort of a logical answer. She did say:

'Christina. . . .' Then after a pause as they both waited, with more hesitation she said, 'Christina Seaton.'

She glanced up quickly at the man holding her hand, saw the amused disbelief in his expression, and angrily jerked at her hand. It was the same as before, clasped tightly and immovable.

'Well, Christina, I think we'd better take you home. Won't someone be very worried about you? You're not very old, you know....' Suddenly the old gaze sharpened, and he asked sharply, 'Just how old are you, my child?'

The form so close to her as it gripped her hand abruptly doubled up with laughter. It was silent laughter, certainly, but that was what it was. And, puzzled, she wondered why.

'Are you worrying that she's about sixteen, Edmond? It wouldn't matter. She really doesn't want publicity any more than I do, I can assure you. But still, how old *are* you ... Christina?'

Deliberately he had hesitated before saying the name. Quite plainly he didn't believe her.

'I'm eighteen—even if I haven't been for long. And I'm quite old enough to look after my own affairs, thank you. All I want to do is leave here.'

'Yes, my dear, you're quite right. She shouldn't be here, Ashley. I'd better take her home to our place, to your Aunt Beth, until we see what's what.'

This time the grasp tightened so cruelly that imperceptibly she winced. His voice, however, when it came, was calm, unhurried, as he answered, 'Oh, no, I don't think so, Edmond. She's not going anywhere. She belongs to me. I found her. She's mine!'

'Yours? You *are* going mad! Don't say such stupid things, my boy. She'd better come with me now. Your aunt and I will sort it all out, and return her to where she belongs.'

'You're not taking her anywhere. She stays here. She knows under what conditions she can leave. Well ...?' Ashley turned, still holding her. 'Am I to take you home, Mystery Girl? Oh, no, I forgot. Am

I to take you home, Christina?'

Both the men stood silent then, waiting her reply, and she stood herself also silent. And unexpectedly, her hand was released.

'There's only one thing wrong with you, Ashley.' Anger coloured with frustration was in the older man's voice, but acceptance came to stand with it, underlying the words. 'All your life you've had everything too easy—too much money, too many willing women, too much of your own way. . . .'

'Oh, no, not everything, Uncle Edmond!' Quietly the sentence came, but there was no mistaking the tone, and the girl beside him glanced up quickly. Surely it hadn't been the nuance of sorrow she had heard in those few words. No, of course not, silly, she admonished herself, seeing in that swift sideways look the image of her companion. With the arrogance, the assured power, and the confidence in what he was . . . and had, surrounding him.

Whatever it had been, actually there or her imagination, was gone now, however. He was laughing at his uncle and Han was murmuring to him in his own language. He was paying attention to it too, the girl who had named herself Christina knew, even while his attention appeared centred entirely upon his uncle.

'No,' he was answering the older man. 'I'll ring Aunt Beth and beg to be let off. I can't leave my guest alone here on her first night, now can I? And as it's only a barbecue my not coming won't upset the numbers.'

What perverse tendency overcame her, she didn't know, but deep down there maybe was the thought that at a barbecue people wandered about and a watch couldn't be kept on a particular person all the time. Perhaps she could slip away, so she said. 'Oh, a barbecue! I love barbecues, Mr—er——?'

'Blythe,' added the man automatically, and then a trifle more slowly, 'Well, of course you could come, my dear . . . if Ashley wishes.'

'Oh, we'll come, if Christina likes barbecues so much. But I'm afraid you'll have to give the pool a miss if the young guests start swimming. They'd be bound to ask you, Christina, what happened to you. Large bandages all round a leg tend to invite comment. One could have anything hidden away beneath it.'

She gazed at him, thinking, I hate you, I really do. Like your uncle said, you've had your own way for far too long. However, she knew there was nothing she could do about it. He was right, and he held the whip hand. The hate blazed up once more as his fingers came out to trail over her bare shoulders where the livid bruise showed dark navy blue with its yellow outer edges. She jerked away.

'You have that formal dinner next Saturday for those Melbourne customers of ours, haven't you, Edmond?' he was saying, the fingers leaving the bruise, but the hand still remaining casually upon her shoulder, and somehow she wasn't game to jerk away a second time, 'so we'll come to that. Dressed up, Christina's bruises won't show. I'll give you time to get home and give my aunt all the gossip, then I'll ring her to confirm Saturday. I know she'll want to ask me about it all again and hear it first hand. Fair enough?' He was smiling at the older man, but it was a sympathetic smile, and he took hold of the elbow nearest him and turned towards the front door. Through slitted, angry eyes she watched, and she did indeed see him take out a key and unlock the door. Blindly she turned away to gaze out through the balcony window towards the glinting ocean, tears desperately held back.

She didn't hear the footsteps coming across the thick carpet; she did hear what was becoming very familiar now—the quick order in what she called in her own mind Chinese.

Hands gently swung her round, but she wouldn't look at him and kept her eyes closed. 'Han is going to get something for that bruise. He should have done so last night, but thought it best to leave well enough alone. When he has done that we'll have lunch.' He moved aside, and Christina felt cool fingers press a pad across the soreness and tape smoothed out to keep it in place.

'There now, go and wash your hands for lunch.' the almost gentle voice said, and without looking at him she began moving down the big room, then feeling his presence behind her doing the same, she felt her back cringe, her shoulders hunch together.

She didn't see the eyes behind her narrow. Eyes that saw that gesture, and, from a dozen years or so away, when his very life had depended on recognising the smallest discrepancy, mark it. At her bedroom door he put out a hand from behind and opened it, and as she turned, he reached up a finger and flicked at a strand of the fair, shining hair. Startled, she glanced up.

'Very nice too,' he told her, white teeth flashing in the brown face.' I always imagined young ladies needed those glossy salons to produce this sort of crowning glory. You appear to have managed it with the solitary help of a comb.'

Not knowing how to answer that, she took refuge in facetiousness. 'Oh, I had more than a comb to help me,' she answered. 'I had thieved shampoo as well.' She received a smile and a flip of his hand as he walked down the hallway—to that lone door in the wall across the corridor. So it was his bedroom—the master bedroom.

In her own, leaning back against the closed door, she put up a hand to her hair. It was easy to handle, but it also needed a good brush—and that she couldn't thieve.

Well, like a kindergarten child, she had been told to go and wash her hands for lunch, so like a kindergarten child she would obey. She went into the bathroom, deciding that she would have to go along with things as they were for the present. She would have to be allowed out of this place some time, and then she would slip away and disappear; this arrogant man wouldn't be able to prevent that. A flush, not of selfconsciousness but of a kind of anger, stained her cheeks as she remembered what he had said to his uncle only a few minutes ago. 'She's not going anywhere. I found her, she's mine.' Well, he would find out she belonged to no one but herself!

Sardonically, she took out the comb and smoothed the pageboy bob, then shrugging, walked out through the living-room to the kitchen. Ashley Carlton was standing gazing out through the glass at the ocean. Han was busy at the other side of the partition.

'Oh, good! Here you are, Christina. Han has prepared some of his country's food for us. Will you try that, or would you prefer a salad?'

I wonder what he'd say if I told him no, thank you to Han's food, and yes, please, I would like a salad? went through her mind. What she did say was, 'Thank you, whatever is prepared. I eat mostly anything.'

It was nearly a silent meal shared by the three of them in the breakfast nook. Christina ate what was placed before her, and after tasting the first mouthful, smiled at the Chinese face opposite, saying, 'It's delicious, Han.'

Her lunch finished, she sat drinking her tea, silent, barely taking in what her companions were discussing, lost in her own thoughts. She jumped, literally, when her host turned and addressed her. 'Well now, Christina, what's on the agenda for this afternoon? You can't spend a glorious Sunday afternoon like this one cooped up indoors. Any suggestions?'

Outraged, she gazed directly into those blue smiling eyes . . . then turned just as swiftly from them. 'I don't know how you have the gall to even ask such a thing! I *can* answer that I wish you'd take me and drop me at the Brisbane bus depot.'

'And how are you going to pay your fare, my dear little mystery girl? I realise there are all sorts of ways of

raising money in this fair golden city, but surely
you . . .?' An interrogative eyebrow climbed.

She could have hit him—with a clenched fist at that.
She had always lived on the Coast. She knew, of course,
its reputation as both a wonderful holiday resort and a
city where anything went for those who wanted it. She
decided to pay him back in his own coin.

'I hadn't thought of that, but of course . . . I expect
I'll have to put on a little extra make-up, though, and
see what I can find, won't I?' And was shocked to
observe those full, sensual lips thin, taking on so
ruthless a line that she pushed her chair back,
frightened at what she had brought about.

'If that's how your mind works, my dear little Miss
Mystery, surely there's no need to go into the city
chasing around. Maybe I can accommodate you up
here.'

More than frightened now by that uncompromising,
ruthless look, she glanced swiftly at both men. Han was
already standing up, calmly gathering together used
plates and cutlery, departing kitchenwards without any
hurry.

Anger came suddenly to dissipate the apprehension.
'There's no need for you to have to accommodate me in
anything, Mr Carlton. Just allow me to go and I'll be
out of your life. And if you must know, I was going to
pawn my watch. It's quite an expensive one, and should
have given me more than enough to pay my fare to
Brisbane. I'll get a job, I'm not afraid of work!' she
finished defiantly.

That ruthless, intimidating look had departed. He
drank from his cup, then said, 'Have you ever worked,
Christina?'

Knowing she must answer, she shook her head.

'Are you still at school, or college?'

Unwilling to say anything that might give him a lead
to her identity, she did not reply, and the man could
see, and read, all the expressions chasing one another

across her countenance. Finally, making up her mind, she told him, 'No. I left school last year and have been doing a secretarial course this one—typewriting and book-keeping.'

'Book-keeping?' He pounced on that one word. 'I can understand the other, but book-keeping ... that's unusual, surely?'

I really do hate him, she thought once again, he notices everything, and her mouth shut mutinously. He waited her out, so she went on, 'A girl has to prepare for some sort of a career in this age of today. I just thought I'd add a little extra.'

'Have you done most of it?' he asked, and was rewarded with a shake of the head.

'But I can type quite well.' Here, for the first time in his acquaintance with her, he noted a mischievous smile come to light up her face—a young girl's smile. 'I hated practising on that damned cardboard mock-up which had to be done before we were allowed near the proper type-writer, so I cheated. . . .' Suddenly she went silent, remembering to whom she was speaking.

But the man before her lids half closed, hooding his eyes and expression, seemed not to have noticed either her words or her abrupt halt.

'What did you mean when you said you could type quite well?'

'That I can type quite well. Not very well, but average. However, I haven't finished my course, so I couldn't get a job in an office. But there are other jobs I could get.'

'Yes ... well. . . .' Her companion had stood up. 'You didn't answer me about what you would like to do this afternoon. Would you like to go down to the beach for a swim? It won't ...' he was adding, then stopped speaking as the silken fair hair swung from side to side. 'No? Then what. . .?' and as she began to answer, he read what she was about to say, and continued himself, 'I'll take you home, Christina, but that's the only place I will take you—apart from any outing in my company which might amuse you. Oh . . .' he had been turning away, but swung back, his voice taking on that slur it sometimes got, 'and I wouldn't get any ideas of slipping away when my back is turned, either. Because then I'd simply ring up a journalist friend of mine and give him the whole story—times and places, and detailed descriptions. The entire story of our meeting would be on the front page tomorrow, because they would be delighted to get a story about me—and what a story! Right off the yellow pages. Still, if that doesn't bother you, by all means walk away when we go out.'

She gazed at him, eyes blazing. She exclaimed, 'I hate you! I wish I were a man and could hurt you. I would!'

He gave a shout of laughter, amused, uninhibited, but all he said was, 'Little termagant! Go and get ready. I'm taking you out. Han. . . .' He turned as Han came to him, smiling. 'Go on off to your family. You're not needed here till tomorrow morning. We can dine out or bring something in for tonight. God knows, there are places enough.' Jaded weariness coloured that slurred tone.

Could they indeed dine out, or bring something in, as if for all the world they were a settled family, thought the girl standing there, and heard Han reply, 'No need for that, Mr Ashley. There is plenty in the fridge for both of you. If you say so, good. I'll get home, my wife will be pleased.'

So Han was married, thought Christina, surprised. Somehow she had imagined there were only the two of them. In this place which seemed to run on oiled wheels she couldn't imagine a wife and family living here. . . . Her thoughts stopped abruptly. And what was the marital status of the owner of this place? She glanced again at him as he stood talking to Han. Tall, bronzed brown by the sun of this region; not handsome in the accepted sense, but attractive . . . oh, yes, that, he certainly was. And that hair, springing from the so

dark countenance, drew all glances to it. The lemon
with its platinum streaks carried a charm all of its own.
Around thirty, or a bit over, she thought, and, by the
look of this place, and his uncle's remarks, well endowed
with this world's goods. He must be married, or—
thinking of present-day customs—probably had been, if
he wasn't now. Her shoulders went up in a shrug. What
did she care about his status?

'Do you want to do what women call "making up
their faces", or are you ready?' An astringent voice
broke into her meditations. Christina turned and left,
thinking as she did that she really did hate him.
Arrogant, overbearing, thinking he could manage the
world! Well, after she found out about something . . .
and please God it wasn't as bad as deep down she knew
it was . . . she would show him . . . show him that he
had no leverage with which to run her life! She cleaned
her teeth, put on lipstick, combed her hair, and with the
small bag slung carelessly upon her shoulder, went to
meet him where he waited at the front door.

CHAPTER THREE

THE sun had passed its zenith when the big car purred up the ramp to surge forward into the heart of Surfers Paradise. It was now on its way westwards to sink behind the foothills beyond. Christina took from her bag the large sunglasses and placed them across her eyes, slipping down a little lower in her seat. The driver of the car had looked carelessly sideways, but seeing that action, the lids had come down half over his eyes. What would normally be thought ordinary behaviour, especially here in the holiday resort of the Gold Coast where fifty per cent of the inhabitants wore them, carried—to the ingrained indoctrination that had been a part off his training years ago—other implications.

His attention back on the traffic as they entered the main Southport road, crowded with vehicles, he stopped at the lights. Giving a more detailed look at his passenger, he saw that she was sitting too low, but at that moment, unexpectedly, a smile tugged at the corner of her lips. Following to where her gaze was directed, he saw in the crowd—because Surfers was always crowded—two bikini-clad girls. With beautiful tanned bodies, with long brown legs and tumbling glossy hair, they strolled carelessly along, giving no heed at all to the glances flung their way—and who would not glance at them, with only their minuscule scraps of coloured material the size of a postage stamp to provide covering.

'Do you wear a bikini, Christina?' her companion asked.

'Yes, of course . . . but not like those,' she answered, then said truthfully, 'I wouldn't look like they do, either. Didn't they have beautiful figures?'

34

'Indeed they did! However ... and I admit this is heresy ... I like my companions, swimming or otherwise, to leave a little more to the imagination. But it takes all sorts. ...'

It did take all sorts, thought the girl, not answering, as she turned to look again out of her own side window. There were all sorts of humanity strolling along the congested footpaths. Elderly tourists a touring bus had just set down, probably for a night out on the coast doing a dinner and show. Youths, jean-clad, or in shorts and bare chests. Young girls in vividly coloured sun-dresses, or tattered jeans and skimpy tied-around tops. Even the occasional business man in his tailored suit, or, like the man beside her, dressed in immaculate slacks and custom-made, short-sleeved shirts.

Through another set of traffic lights and they had turned away from the bustling throngs, and were travelling westwards up towards the foothills beyond the coastline. Christina lay back, seeing nothing of the beautiful homes and colourful gardens through which they were passing, lost in thoughts that were neither beautiful nor colourful.

Only another ten minutes or so of driving in the swiftly moving vehicle and they had turned through a gateway in a chain-wire fence, passing stack upon stack of sawn timber. Christina wondered how it would ever be used up, even with all the building going on in the town they had just left. She said as much, forgetting for the moment about her companion and the reason she was here.

'It will be used, with more coming to join it all the time,' he was answering idly. Then he had opened his door to step out, and when hers was pulled wide, she placed a hand in the one stretched out to help her automatically as if it were the natural thing to do— again she didn't see the expression in the man's eyes change.

They had slid to a stop, not over among those giant

stacks of timber, but before a small office building, lawn-enclosed with a barrier of thick-foliaged trees between it and the mill. 'Wait here, Christina, while I find Fenton,' said Ashley Carlton, and made off towards the mill.

He didn't have to try to find anyone. A large grey-haired man had apparently seen the car arrive and with a hand half raised in salutation was heading towards them. Her companion walked forward. They stood, the conversation going back and forth, then both turned, heading back.

'This is Alan Fenton, Christina, our mill manager. Miss Christina Seaton, Alan.'

'Mr Fenton,' acknowledged Christina, returning his friendly smile.

'Happy to meet you, Miss Seaton,' the man replied in a slow drawl, and Christina liked him right away.

'Christina is the daughter of one of Aunt Beth's friends and is up here for a while,' came the unblushing lie from over her head, 'and I'd better get her back,' he was continuing in the same breath. 'I've got a few more jobs to finish, now I've got that little trouble you've had here settled to our satisfaction.'

The older man shook his head, and Christina didn't know if it was in admiration or censure. He said, 'I'm damned glad I'm on your side of the fence, Ashley. You're a ruthless ... Oh, sorry,' he swung round to apologize to Christina as he cut off the epithet.

She felt like saying, 'Be my guest'. It was exactly what she thought of Ashley Carlton herself. However, she was being helped into the front seat of the Jaguar, and dropping into his own place, Ashley leaned out a laughing countenance. 'You're too solemn, Alan. Come down yonder and I'll take you to lunch one day next week.'

'No fear, you won't! I'm not one of your executive types who take two or three hours over a meal. I'm lucky if I get half an hour to swallow mine without one interruption.'

'That's your own fault. You're the boss—and the best mill manager around. Any firm would be only too happy to snaffle you and give you two hours for lunch, if we were ever silly enough to let you go. Now come down for lunch on Wednesday. That's an order!' If the Jaguar could be said to be so ill-bred as to leap forward with gravel spurting from beneath its wheels, that was what it did. Slowing down a little along the winding road, it pulled to a stop on a wide shoulder, and the driver turning to look at Christina.

'How about telling me the story of your life Christina? ... if Christina is really your name, which I beg leave to doubt. I can help you, you know,' and as she still remained silent he leant over and took hold of her hand. But she shook her head and from where it hung downwards he heard her say, 'I can't ... I can't....'

The silence lasted for another long minute, so he placed her hand back again and in an entirely different voice said, 'You liked Alan Fenton, didn't you? How would you like to work for him?'

That brought her head up. 'Work for him? How can I?'

'You told me you can type. The mill needs a junior. But I'm warning you that if you do say yes, you will be accorded no privileges. You'll have to do as you're told and be the general dogsbody. I don't think somehow that that's what you've been used to.'

Christina ignored the last sentence, pondering on the first one. This mill was out of the mainstream of the Coast, and also at its northern end, not the southern one where she couldn't have contemplated being. And she had to do something until.... She wished she knew.... A shiver passed through her and Ashley's voice broke roughly into her silence.

'Well?'

'Yes, please,' she said—and wasn't near enough to feel the sudden relaxation of his body. 'I'll have to find somewhere to stay, though.'

'For instance, where?' she was interrupted.

Puzzled, she looked at him, wondering at the tone.

'Well, of course I will, won't I?'

'What's wrong with where you're staying now?'

'Don't be silly, Mr Carlton. Of course I can't stay there!'

'Why?' Uncompromising the one word came.

'Because . . . because I couldn't, because it wouldn't be suitable.' She couldn't bring herself to say why it wouldn't be suitable. He should damn well know why himself.

Again he used the word 'Why'. 'Why wouldn't it be suitable, Christina? Is it that you'll be sharing a flat with a man—actually, with two men? But it's done all the time these days. No one even remarks on it.'

She knew he was right, and that the situation probably worked out. But she herself wouldn't be doing it. Only because she wouldn't like it—not because she objected to it being done. And that sharing didn't occur in penthouses like the one the man beside her occupied. It was entered into on a money-saving basis.

She said tartly, 'I'm afraid I couldn't afford your accommodation, Mr Carlton. A third of the shared rent on that unit would most likely be more than a whole week's pay of mine.'

Again, as she had seen him do on another occasion, he doubled up with laughter. 'Well then,' he said when he was upright once more, 'we'll have to see if you can pay your rent in other ways. What do you say to that proposition, my mystery girl?'

She wondered what he would do if she turned round on him and accepted that outrageous suggestion, and then her mouth went tightly closed, as she remembered his demeanour when she had tried that game once before.

Flinging out her hands helplessly, she told him, 'It's not possible. You know it's not!'

'I know nothing of the kind, but we'll leave it for the

time being. Something will be managed. For now . . . I know I suggested a swim earlier—however, with your leg and shoulder not as healthy as they could be, that isn't really practical. Would you care to just stroll arround Surfers and see the sights for an hour or so?'

A negative shake of the fair shining head answered him, not definite, just uncaring.

'I'm a member of the Twin Service Club at the other end of the Coast. How about a drink there? It's always crowded and lively.'

This time the shake of the head was much more emphatic.

'I must say, Christina, you're a hard girl to please. I know—we'll go to the Tweed River golf club. That's in New South Wales and they have poker machines there. You can play them if you feel so inclined, and then we'll have afternoon tea. How about that?' He made to reach out to turn a switch, but breathless words stopped him.

'Please, Mr Carlton, I don't feel like doing anything like that. My leg is hurting a bit, so I'd rather not go running around.'

'All right, then. We'll go home,' he said, and the narrowed eyes held satisfaction. So this mystery girl of his didn't want to go south. Purposely he had dropped in different localities. Now, at least, he knew which one she didn't want to go to. He didn't realise, however, that his own words had hit sharply.

'We'll go home,' he had said. God, home!

They swung down the winding road, the car just cruising, and only silence encircled them both. However, on entering the built-up area, Ashley said, 'We'll be passing a building site that I have interests in. Do you mind if I stop for a minute, Christina?' Casually said, the words could have been addressed to a young girl belonging to the friend of his aunt's that he had described her as.

She saw when they drove into the kerb that they had stopped before a very large area indeed, from which, although it was Sunday, rubble was being collected and driven away. A big old building must have been demolished, probably to make room for an even larger one. Watching idly, Christina saw her host, or captor, or whatever, speaking to a man who had come to meet him. Whatever the business had been, it didn't take long before he was back and slipping into his seat.

'Would you mind, Christina,' he began a trifle breathlessly from his enforced run down a steep incline, 'if I call in at yet another site?'

'Would it matter if I did mind?' she enquired sweetly. 'I can't remember any of my other desires being granted while I've known you.'

'Yes, certainly it would matter if you think I'm being discourteous while I run round on my own business; and of course I'll take you home and come back. As for the other, I've told you at least on two different occasions the remedy that will free you from my penthouse.'

Unwilling to hear that cold, curt voice, when it had remained so different all the rest of the afternoon, Christina turned her head away, but replied in a polite tone with no colour at all in it, 'Please go about your business. I'll be quite happy waiting in the car.'

For a moment longer he didn't move, then he put the Jaguar into motion and they moved again towards the heart of the town. Making herself speak—anything to break this bleak atmosphere—she asked, 'Do you construct buildings, Mr Carlton?'

'No, Miss Seaton, our firm doesn't actually do the building. Big construction companies do that. But my company has an interest in the ones where we provide the land. And of course, as we have that, we see that our timber, our bricks, our cement, and our glass, are used.'

'Do you own land here, then?' Her hand went out to gesture to the streets around them.

'I do. My father bought acres of beachfront land all

along the Coast years ago before it was caught up in the
tourist boom. That was before the war . . . before I was
born, even. You know, life's funny, Christina,'
apparently her companion had forgotten his sarcastic
rejoinder of 'Miss Seaton' in answer to her 'Mr
Carlton', because he was saying, 'My father went all
through the Second World War and was in the thick of
some of the worst battles of it, but surviving it all, he
came back home, married, had me, then he and my
mother went on a trip to Europe. Nothing so mundane
as a plane crash killed them—no, it was a bloody
earthquake in one of the Balkan countries that one had
never heard of. . . .' The man stopped speaking for a
moment, then quietly continued.

'So, all that land was tied up until I came of age. My
lawyer, my accountants, Uncle Edmond, nearly had
apoplexy. The land was jumping and they couldn't sell
a piece of it. They didn't realise then that it was going
to keep going up. And of course, in those days twenty-
one was the age of majority, not eighteen, as it is now.
So I spent my schooldays over there,' he pointed to
some buildings hidden in clusters of greenery, 'and my
holidays with Aunt Beth and Uncle Edmond.

'And yet once more, waiting patiently—or rather
impatiently—for me to be able to sign releases, again
they found themselves stymied.' Here, an almost ironic
smile parted the lips of the man speaking so absently to
her. 'Because I was called up for national service and
sent to Vietnam to spend my twenty-first birthday over
there—and my twenty-second. My twenty-third was
looming before I finally got home. A lot of my land has
gone now, but it was the pieces in Surfers Paradise itself
that brought in the millions . . . as if I cared!'

The girl looked quickly sideways and up, as she heard
that last softly spoken sentence, and the tone in which it
had been uttered. But whether he had been aware of it
or not, she didn't know, because immediately he was
stepping from the stationary car. She watched him enter

a half-finished high-rise building, then gazed carelessly around. Suddenly her body tensed and she looked quickly at the building through which Ashley Carlton had disappeared.

She put out a hand swiftly, wondering abruptly if the door was locked from the dashboard. It wasn't, and she unlatched it, getting out. Another glance around and she was walking briskly back the way they had come for a hundred yards or so, to step into a public telephone booth.

Inside, eyes shadowed again, hands beginning to tremble, she took the silver coin from her change purse and began to dial. She needed to check no numbers, and a shaking finger rolled the digits round. She heard the telephone ring at the other end and waited breathlessly for a voice to answer—but the phone only returned the ringing tone. She stood, allowing it to ring until she knew it wouldn't be answered, then hung up the receiver.

The tingling sound of the unused coin returning didn't register. Was the no answer a bad sign, or a good sign? was going through her mind. She wished she knew.

A passing figure reflected in the glass of the cabinet brought her attention back to the moment, to this other quandary, and gazing through the glass she saw the Jaguar, and, standing in the doorway opposite, Ashley Carlton in conversation with another man. Pushing the door open quickly, Christina walked back to take her place in the car. For a further minute the owner of it continued his discussion, then he had turned, and waiting as a car sped screeching past, had opened his door and was sitting beside her. He didn't mention the fact that she had been out—and he must have seen her. She remained silent.

The big car purred forward and in two minutes they had swung into the underground car park of their own building. Ashley came round and opened her door, unlocked the elevator, and the unit, accomplishing it all without a word uttered.

Inside, he walked towards the big TV set and switched it on. 'Okay, Christina, I need my afternoon tea. Have I got to get it myself, or can you make yourself useful for your bed and board?'

Startled, she gazed back at him. He *was* serious. 'I could get it, but I don't know where anything is,' she told him.

'Well, now's the time to see how you're going to make out in the big, bad world. If you can't find your way among Han's gadgets to make a simple cup of tea and find something to eat with it, I don't give you much chance.'

The look she gave him was a glare. He laughed, and an eyebrow climbed. 'Well?' he asked.

Flouncing was the only word to describe the way she turned and threw her bag on the sofa. But in Han's kitchen she hesitated, then told herself not to be stupid. Anyone could switch on a kettle and make a pot of tea. So, straightening her back, she took hold of a silver kettle, placed it beneath a long chrome tap and turned it on. A smile came as the water gushed out hot and with confidence now she turned the switch.

Next came the search in cupboards for the teapot. She found it, not in a cupboard, but on a silver tray—a tall white fluted pot with milk jug and sugar basin to match, absolutely austere with only a fine ring of silver around the top for ornamentation. Lifting the lot down, she rinsed out the pot with hot water, then looked round for the tea. That was easy—among a set of canisters with tea marked on it. Good; two teaspoons for them ... her thoughts stilled abruptly. For them! She would have to watch herself. Ashley might be keeping her here because he had run over her, but even without ... without ... she would never come within his orbit. 'And one for the pot,' she muttered to herself determinedly. The kettle whistled, and she poured the boiling water.

Then, hands on hips, she stood in the centre of the kitchen, gazing about her. The fridge provided the thinnest smoked salmon sandwiches she had ever seen, clad in Cellophane, and then she began opening everything she could find with a lid on it. 'Eureka!' she exclaimed in triumph, and pulled out a cake—not a creamy sponge, but a dark fruit one. Yes, this looked like that man out there. Cream cake didn't seem his style at all.

Carrrying the tray, she marched out to the big living room and dumped it on a small inlaid table beside where he was stretched out in a deep chair watching a golf replay. From under his lashes he looked up lazily and said, 'Oh, good girl! Milk and one sugar for me, please!'

Christina poured his tea milk and sugared, then placed it in a long brown hand held out for it. Moving the sandwiches closer to him, she filled her own cup, then picking it up, walked out to the balcony with it. Dropping on to one of the white patio chairs, she sat sipping, her gaze abstractedly on the rushing, restless blue-green waves far beneath her. She didn't notice the man studying the countenance turned sideways to him, taking in the lonely, unmoving figure she presented. She didn't see him rise and, replacing his own cup, pick up the tray to move out on the balcony as well. He dropped the tray on the matching table beside her.

The sound broke into her isolation, and she gazed without comprehension at the tray first, then up at him. He was, however, leisurely picking up his cup, and taking a sandwich, he said, 'We'll have our tea and then we'll talk about you and tomorrow.'

Silently he went on with his meal, demolishing the sandwiches, ignoring the cake, then leaning comfortably back, he began, 'Now—I'll go and ring Edmond. It will look better if he sees Fenton about the job. There's no

need for you to be associated with me. About clothes—
I take it that you haven't any ... have no suitcase
stashed away that you can collect?' Receiving no
answer, he continued smoothly, 'You'd better go with
Han up to Sundale in the morning and buy the
rudiments of a wardrobe; you'll only need necessities
for the time being. An office dress to work in and the
requisites for underneath it ...' he grinned as she
turned her head away. 'Don't be a prude, Christina. In
today's world what's left to wonder about, taking in
consideration the advertisements on TV and the
newspapers. So here,' he pulled out a wallet and
extracted two notes to lay them on the table beside her
cup, and added, 'It's little enough, but the way you go
on, I expect you'd rather not take it, except that you
have to. Right?'

Christina gazed down at the two fifty-dollar notes as
if they were two-headed cobras, both rearing to strike,
and thrust her chair back, repudiation in the very act.

'Look, Christina, you can give it to me back—and I
tell you, I'm getting sick and tired of disagreements
every time something comes up. What in the hell is
that?' A thin brown finger flicked at the notes. 'That
wouldn't buy one decent dress, and you still wouldn't
get much change out of it for an ordinary one. I
know. . . .'

'I'll just bet you do,' interrupted Christina sarcas-
tically, then as suddenly capitulated. 'Very well, I'll
accept it, and I'll return it if ... when ... I get a pay
cheque.' She was thinking, however, I won't be at the
mill office long enough to get a pay cheque. Before
then, I'll find out about. . . . One way or another I'll
know. But I'm not going to dwell on that now. I'll ring
again tomorrow.

'Have you finished your tea?' she enquired politely,
and was rewarded with an exasperated shrug of the
shoulders. So piling the used dishes on the tray, she
went to pick it up, when it was taken from her hands.

She followed both it and its owner to the kitchen, where
he placed it on a bench with more than a little force as
if taking out on it the annoyance her reply had
engendered in him. Then, turning, he bumped into her.

For only a minute they stood thus, but unexpectedly,
a new dimension flowed around them. Christina felt the
hard body against hers and was suddenly breathless.
Unable to speak, unable. . . .

It was the man who abruptly moved back, and when
he spoke it was in a different tone from any she had
heard hitherto—deliberate, curt to the point of
rudeness. 'I'm going out for a while, I'll only be gone an
hour or so. There are books in a bookcase in the study
just off the dining room. And, of course, the TV if you
want it. But a rest wouldn't go amiss, by the look of
you.' The last sentence came harshly. He was gone.

Christina stood there and watched him walk down
the long room, unlock the door and walk through—and
still she stood. What in the name of goodness had
happened? Even if she had left school only last year, she
wasn't a silly schoolroom miss. She had been educated
here on the Coast and had led the life of any
comfortably-off young girl, had partied and danced,
gone to swimming-pool raves and barbecues, had been
taken out by partners and brought home by them, been
kissed goodnight—and had laughed away the endea-
vours to make the kiss oh, so much more.

Her girl friends had teased her, and told it around
that she got her romance from books. But that was not
the case, she defended herself now. She had been liked
and had liked in return, but she had thought there was
time enough for the heavy scene. After all, she was only
seventeen, going on eighteen, and there was a career to
get involved in. Perhaps one day. . . .

Well, she admonished herself sardonically now, she
had better not allow herself to think that perhaps that
day had arrived. Just thinking of Ashley Carlton with
his penthouse, his business, his . . . mistresses, was

enough to show her that. Because he did have his mistresses. Hadn't his uncle said how beautiful the current one was? No, had been. And implying that that affair was over, Ashley had added the words 'for now, anyway'. There probably would be others, but she wouldn't be among them. As soon as she could find out, and the facts would have to come out one way or another soon, she would get out of this place. But . . . her eyes closed and she felt again that body along the length of hers; that feeling of caring for nothing else except having it there.

Violently, she opened her eyes and, turning, deliberately began to clean up the afternoon tea debris. She washed and rinsed and dried up, returning used articles to where they belonged. She passed the dining room from which she had been told a study with books opened out, and walked straight on to her own room. Inside, with the door closed, she threw down the quilt and, lying face down, turned her face to the pillow.

Some time later the sobs grew less hard, a more even breathing taking over. Gradually her head sank deeper into the softness beneath it, and, not knowing, she drifted into the sleep of nervous exhaustion. As the evening shadows began to creep through the wide glass windows, she didn't hear the owner of the place arriving home, go through the whole apartment, then come quietly down the corridor to stand listening outside her door. He raised a hand and tapped softly. After a moment of silent waiting, he knocked again. Receiving no answer, he turned the knob, and a look of satisfaction passed across his face. So she hadn't locked it!

Gently opening the door the smallest slit, he glanced through, to see the sprawled, unmoving figure on the bed. Walking across, his progress making no sound on the thick carpet, he came to the bedside and stood gazing down. The fair, shining hair was half over a face pressed into the pillow; it didn't hide, however, the tear stains that showed their passage down her cheeks. For a moment longer he looked, then turned, and just as quietly made his way out. His face was not carrying the normal pleasant casualness it usually held, however. A scowl, deep and horrendous, turned the face into a ruthless mask.

CHAPTER FOUR

As they had done yesterday morning, Christina's eyes opened on the same room. No puzzlement marred that glance this daybreak, though. She came awake immediately and knew at once where she was.

The room was not in dimness either. As she had been occupying it last night, Han had not come to draw the curtains and fold down the quilt. Glinting, gleaming, dancing across to her from the big windows, rays from a sun just risen over the edge of the world sent their good-morning. Outside, in the early light, the ocean had the sheen of lapis lazuli, but the sky was not showing its normal brazen blueness; it held almost a luminous quality of pearl over cerulean, and somehow the glory of the new morning made the world look a little brighter to her.

Her gaze alighted on the crumpled dress and bikini lying on the floor beside her bed and her brow furrowed. She remembered waking some time during the night, and half asleep, fuzzily aware that it was late, slipped them off and donned the pyjama top from under her pillow, then automatically pulling the covers around her shoulders had fallen asleep again at once.

Now she slid out of bed, but instead of padding barefooted across to the window, she walked purposely bathroomwards. Again automatically, she bathed with a leg hanging sideways, and trying not to wet the pad on her shoulder. As she gazed at the awkward angle of her leg and foot, suddenly the funny side of her being this way in the bath struck her and she gave a chuckle— an uninhibited, girlish little laugh.

Picking up the enormous sponge, she squeezed it and washed the exposed foot and leg, then, 'Oh, blow it!'

she cried as she slipped, and her shoulder and Han's dressing went whoosh! under the water. Rising like a nymph from the soapsuds, she quickly dried herself, looked with distaste at the already worn clothes she would have to put on, but consoled herself that there would be fresh ones this morning, even if they were obtained with borrowed money. A quick flick of lipstick, a comb through her hair, and with shoulders straightened, she went out to meet whoever was waiting—and met Han almost at her door, carrying a tray with hospital-smelling paraphernalia on it.

He marched straight before her into the bathroom and placed his burden upon the vanity table, pulling out, as he did so, the small chair for her. However, he didn't at once sit on the edge of the bathtub, and Christina felt cool fingers pull down the top of her strapless dress the merest fraction. Swabbed with some pungent lotion, the plaster covering the pad on her bruised shoulder was carefully eased off—not ripped quickly, as it had sometimes been from childhood hurts.

'There, it doesn't look too bad now, does it?' asked the bland, friendly, hardly accented voice. And gazing sideways into the mirror, Christina saw that though the inner core of the bruise was still coloured and angry-looking, the wound itself had receded inwardly and was not half as big. The same cool fingers were massaging ointment smoothly into it, then the dress was patted up the infinitesimal fraction it had been lowered, and Han said,

'There's no need to put a dressing on it, it doesn't show a great deal. And now for this leg of yours.' The bandage was unrolled, the gauze pad gently uplifted. And again Han smiled. Glancing at her leg, Christina didn't think there was too much to smile about. It, like the shoulder, didn't seem to cover such a large surface as it had previously done. But in the middle it was all pus and bloody-looking.

'It's fine,' said her doctor, reading the expression

showing on her face, and reaching into his tray of tricks, he picked up a glass phial. Gently he shook powder over the entire surface of the wound, then carefully applied a small dressing. 'Definitely healing,' he said. 'Only a few days more ... but you can go swimming with it now. It will just do it good.' Casually he washed his hands at the basin, wiped them fastidiously dry on a towel from his tray, and picking it up was departing purposefully.

'I'll get your breakfast, Miss Christina. Mr Ashley has already left, and we are to go shopping, you know.'

Following the retreating back, Christina said to it a little breathlessly, as if wanting to make some of her own wishes known. 'I don't eat a big breakfast, Han. Just tea and toast and some orange juice if you have it.'

They had it! It was already standing in a bowl of crushed ice, a tall glass of freshly squeezed juice. She sat on the chair Han had pulled forward and taking up the glass, sipped, while Han moved on into the kitchen. She sat drinking, wondering how best to begin the words she wanted to say to Han. Her reverie was interrupted. At least he had taken some notice of her words, she thought. Only a boiled egg was set before her, accompanied by toast. And as he poured the tea she gave a glance of recognition to the tall white pot.

'Han,' she asked, cutting off the top of her egg, 'why does Mr Carlton want me to stay here? It seems such a strange thing for him to be doing. ...' Her words trailed off. She couldn't say to Han that there was a very obvious reason why a man should detain a young girl in his apartment. She knew absolutely that that wasn't the reason in this case. Because why on earth should it be? He had no need for such subterfuge. Being what he was, and who he was, he would have his pick of beautiful women ... willing women.

'Mr Ashley ran over you with his car,' answered the bland voice. 'Perhaps he wants to be sure in his own mind that you have taken no harm from it.'

Christina felt like saying, 'Don't be stupid, Han!' but one couldn't be rude to this polite, smiling man. She ate her breakfast.

Plummeting down in the express lift, they walked past the opened garage, which was empty of its owner's vehicle, and Han unlocked a Holden station-wagon. Back through what was becoming familiar territory they drove, but then Han turned away from the bustling, crowded section of the coast. He drove comfortably along and then concentrated on negotiating the busy lanes into the vast shopping centre that was their destination.

Locking the car, he spoke for the first time. 'You won't find your way back among all these cars, Miss Christina, so I will take you to the department store, and,' he raised a hand to glance at his wristwatch, 'I'll give you two hours and then return for you at this entrance. Will that be all right? I have to do some shopping myself for the unit.' He waved a hand as she nodded and walked away.

She watched him go, then turned into the store, asking an attendant behind an enquiry counter where the public telephones were, and marched off as they were pointed out.

Again she put in the ten cents and dialled, and again her legs felt like rubber that didn't want to support her. And also, as before, the dialling tone rang and rang. This time when the silver coin fell through as she replaced the receiver, she retrieved it. She might want it another time. She knew she could ring the office; she knew she should. But she would have to give her name to be put through, and if. . . . Pushing her leaning form from off the glass behind her, she stepped away from the phone and decided determinedly to get on with the reason for her being here.

Underclothes first. She remembered Ashley's astringent words about them when he was deciding she had to buy a new wardrobe, and suddenly a kind of grin

etched itself about her lips, lightening the sombreness of
her demeanour. Half a dozen pair of briefs were thrown
into the trolley she had collected, some bras following
in their turn. She had never actually done this kind of
shopping before. At school, she had been bought for,
and after leaving, had been taken to a boutique and had
been waited on. This was fun, she decided as she made
for the shoe racks. Only able to afford one pair, she
chose a pair of white strapped sandals with medium
high heels. Just the thing for work, not too dressy, and
not too casual either.

Yes, this looked like office wear, she decided, and
added a well-cut, straight coffee-coloured skirt, to her
growing pile. Pushing the trolley before her, she went
up and down the aisle searching for tops. And yes, that
yellow one would do, she told herself, taking from its
hanger the cool lemon blouse, also adding one in white,
pintucked and laced. Another dress for the office, an
autumn-toned jersey, simply cut with small sleeves and
a scooped neckline. She always thought these colours
suited her mostly, with her amber eyes and fair hair.

She roughly costed up the total. Things were not
expensive, but they certainly added up. What she had
bought for the office would do for the day or two she
might be there. . . . She shrugged. She would take the
days as they came, and she dropped into the steadily
growing pile a towelling strapless yellow shift for basic
wear. She didn't need to try anything on; she knew her
size.

'Oh!' It was a mutter to herself. Passing a rack which
was only now being filled, she paused. The cheeky little
dresses were so attractive—white, with blue or red or
yellow trim, and with a wide, deep sailor collar. 'A bit
short, though,' she muttered. But this one she would
have to try on. It was loose to just above the knees,
then pleated . . . she hadn't ever worn anything like it
before.

There should be enough money, she thought, with a

glance at the price, but it wouldn't leave her much over, and she might need money. Defiantly she took hold of one—and not a yellow-trimmed one, either. She chose a blue, and went to the fitting room. Leaving her laden trolley with the attendant, she went into the small booth and tried the dress on. Looking into the full-length mirror, she smiled. This new modern look certainly did something for her, in fact, more than something. Not that she looked beautiful ... suddenly she knew what had brought that thought to her mind. Of course she wasn't beautiful. Of course she didn't expect anyone to think she was. She took off the dress and donned her own, thinking that thank goodness, she could soon dispense with the bikini as underclothes. She would change them as soon as she got home. Home! There she went again. Oh, well. . . .

She made her way to the check-out counter and as the girl began punching her buttons, she turned and smiled—one girl to another. 'You're certainly replenishing your wardrobe,' the girl commented.

'Yes, and I needed to,' replied Christina, smiling back, but thinking ... and you'll never know how much I needed to!

She found she had just over five dollars change ... she would manage. She wasn't going anywhere, she knew that! Now she wanted to stay where she was, until ... and she refused to think of that other dimension which had flared around two still figures yesterday as they stood in a kitchen last evening.

She found Han waiting when she neared the entrance he had designated, loaded down with her carry-bags. He laughed when he saw her, and reached out a hand to relieve her of some of them. 'All finished?' he asked.

'Yes,' she replied, adding, 'and all nearly broke again!'

'It doesn't matter,' was all the answer she received.

Back up the lift and waiting for the door to be unlocked, Christina glanced round the small foyer, deep-carpeted, watercolours on the walls, and felt, as she preceded Han into the beautiful Eastern living room, that she *was* coming home, and knew absolutely how happy she was at being able to do so.

Waving to Han, she turned in the direction of her own room to begin folding away her gleanings of the morning into drawers and wardrobes. Discarding the exclusive, imported dress and bikini, she pulled on briefs and bra and the yellow towelling knock-about. Reaching down for them, she went out to discover if there was so mundane a room as a laundry in this palace in the sky.

Han was performing what she had just been engaged upon, bending down to a cupboard. Upright again, he glanced at her and at the clothes in her hand. He said, 'The laundry, Miss Christina. It's through here.' He backed through a wooden-slatted swing door; the kind one saw in western movies giving way to an old-fashioned saloon bar. This one, however, showed gleaming, tiled in white, and held everything necessary for use in a laundry.

'Can you work the washing machine, and the dryer?' asked Han, and receiving a nod, threw an arm out to cover the room, saying, 'Be my guest, then,' as he returned to the kitchen.

Christina didn't use the machine, hand-washing and double-rinsing her dress. Hanging it on a line across one of the corners, she then washed and pegged up her bikini beside it.

Returning through a kitchen empty of Han, she was walking to her own quarters when she suddenly halted and turned into the dining room. There was a room opening off it, and inside, she found the book case she had been told about. Ignoring the desk with its stacks of papers and folders, its filing cabinet alongside, the big windows providing almost a searchlight with which to work at it, she made straight to the books. A shelf full of technical stuff and reference volumes ran across the top. Then probably every modern best-seller occupied shelf after shelf—history, espionage, mystery, biographies. Her glance moved along, looking for something she herself might like to read.

None of the vivid-jacketed love stories she might like were there. But of course there wouldn't be, the sarcastic reflection went through her mind. The man this place belonged to would most likely have no time for reading about romantic affairs, *he* would be too busy making them happen. But surely there was something that might interest her. In the end, she picked what looked, from its colourful cover, an historical love story, while promising to buy herself some paperbacks the first chance she got.

With it clutched in one hand she made her way from the study, not stopping to admire the works of art scattered about as she walked back. However, in her own room, lying in a chair by the window, the book on her lap, she didn't even turn the first page, just lay back, eyes closed, thinking ... thinking of what she had left behind, but also, too, without volition, thinking of Ashley Carlton. How his eyes laughed when he was amused, and to the contrary, how black they could turn, when he was angry. How his amazingly lemon-fair hair drew one's glance, outstanding as it was against the bronzed tan of his skin. How. . . . She gave herself a shake. Was she mad, thinking like this about him? She closed her eyes and leaned her head against the chairback. For some time she lay there, so immobile that the room could have been empty. She nearly jumped from the chair when a soft knock came upon her door.

'Come and eat, Miss Christina,' called a cheerful voice. 'Only a sandwich.'

It might have been Han's idea of only a sandwich, but it wasn't hers. They both ate at the table on the balcony, and carefully looking for a place where she could get her mouth around, Christina enquired, 'What in the name of goodness have you got in them, Han?'

'Eat it and find out,' was the only reply she received. They sat comfortably together, gazing down on an ocean spilling white-capped upon the sands below.

'Would you like a swim, Miss Christina?' asked Han, breaking into the silence which had lasted for some time. 'I think the sea would be desirable, although we have two pools in our grounds. Salt water will be best for your leg, however. Oh . . .' he paused suddenly, 'tell me,' he began again, 'can you swim? I wouldn't dare come back here if I lost you away out there.'

A grin answered him; a youthful grin, uninhibited. 'Yes, I can swim, quite well. In fact, like my typing I can do it quite well, but not brilliantly. It's all right for me to go swimming, then?' an enquiring eyebrow lifted.

'Of course. Go and change into your swimming gear. I'll be with you as soon as I have cleared this away. No, leave that, Miss Christina,' he added, as she began to pack her plate and cup.

Christina replaced the crockery she had picked up, and glancing at him, wondered if she could ask him not to call her miss Christina all the time, then shrugging, she turned away, thinking better of it. He knew what he was doing, and she wouldn't be here that long.

Strolling back from their swim, she turned impulsively to him, saying, 'I did enjoy it, Han. I realise things haven't changed, but being forced to keep afloat in that rough surf makes the situation seem not so difficult somehow. . . .' She hesitated a moment, then decided to dwell only in the present for the time being.

She followed him upstairs, and turned to smile at him as he shut the penthouse door behind them . . . and didn't realise there was another presence occupying the long room. Han did. 'You're home early, Mr Ashley,' he called down its length. 'We've just been braving the ocean . . . and you will have to get that wet dressing off your leg, Miss Christina,' he was adding.

All smiles wiped from her face, she stood waiting, as

that figure rose slowly from his chair and walked towards them. That unknown dimension was encircling her whole body again, and as he came close, she had to physically force herself to stand still, not to step back from him.

A finger flicked at the yellow shift, and he said, paraphrasing a sentence he had said to her once before at the door of her room, 'And not very nice, too.'

'It hasn't got to be nice; it's only a knockabout covering. Hundreds of girls wear them everywhere ... every day. Her tone was defensive.

'I know!' Flatly, she was answered in two words, and she was left in no doubt what that tone meant.

'And what else did you buy with that vast amount of money you had?' the amused voice asked.

Defiantly remaining there, twelve or so inches distance from him, although wanting to turn and run, she answered, her tone as flat as his had been a moment ago, her eyes resting on the chest level with them, not looking up, 'I bought two office outfits—no, three,' she amended, remembering that there were two blouses to go with the skirt. 'Some necessities,' she added, and thought, if he gets that grin on his face, so help me, I really will hit him! But glancing upwards suddenly, she saw his face was quite grave, even if there was, far back, a glint in the so blue eyes.

'And,' she continued, wanting to get the story out of the way, 'a pair of shoes, a dress for going out—if I'm allowed to go out—or to change into for the evening.. That's the lot!'

'God! That's the lot! How did you manage to get all that? I expected one dress and a pair of shoes, some briefs, and,' here he looked directly at her before adding, 'other underclothes.'

Before the answer he saw coming could eventuate, he continued hurriedly, 'I'm pleased you had enough to purchase a dress for, as you explain, going out, because we are going out to dine tonight. And I don't expect an office dress would do anything for your ego. However, I would have been entirely satisfied for you to wear the one in which I found you. . . .'

'Oh, anything to keep you satisfied, Mr Carlton. My sole aim in life would be to do that.' Vitriol dripped from her words.

Ashley laughed. 'Did I tell you once before you were a little termagant? However, I'll give you my view on the new dress when you're ready. Seven o'clock!' He reached out a casual finger to touch her cheek and suddenly they were standing in a field charged with electricity, caught immobile in an enclosed space with the crackle of static encircling them. Unable to do otherwise, she looked directly at him—into eyes that held a brightness she had never before encountered. Then, abruptly, she was gazing into a blank face devoid of any expression, lids having fallen to hood completely that piercing brilliance. For a minute longer they stood as if caught in an instant tableau, rigid, unmoving, then suddenly the man had swung on his heels. All she was aware of was a back, straight-held, carrying stiffness in a carriage where before the normal characteristic had been only one of indolent casualness.

He disappeared, and still she stood. Then, with no sign of the man's quick departure, she turned, and with dragging footsteps went to her own room. Across at the window she remained for a long time, gazing out bleakly, seeing nothing of the far-flung vista of sea and landscape, of buildings that added their own effect as they reared skywards to arch against cerulean infinity, less distinctive now as the shadows of early evening began to encroach. Almost dusk now, in half an hour it would be full dark.

That thought penetrated the daze in which she was locked. Ashley had said they were to dine out. That was before . . . but he hadn't rescinded the order, or sent Han to do so. She had better get away from this place, she knew that, but now . . . now that she didn't want to, that man out there would be probably wishing her away. She sighed. He had the means in his own hands.

But for now, she had her leg to do—and nothing to do it with. She walked towards the bathroom—and there was Han's tray on the vanity table. He had told her while returning from the beach that she could manage for herself now. She was just to keep it clean and apply the brown powder night and morning.

She hung the despised towelling dress away, slipped out of bikini and under the shower. Out and dried, she found it simple to ease off the wet dressing. Carefully she followed the pattern that Han had used, while being, she told herself, a little more heavy-handed with the healing powder than she had meant to be. Nevertheless, the covering didn't look too clumsy, she reflected, as she patted it into place. Not as neat as the one performed by Han. Still, her shoulder bruise had deteriorated to a faint yellow patch and was hardly noticeable at all.

Made up and dressed, she glanced at herself all ways in the long mirror. If he said 'and not very nice, too,' this time, she muttered to herself, she really would hit him. Because, without flattering herself, she knew she looked more than 'very nice'. The short dress swung in pleats just at the top of her knees, the blue trim, the wide sailor collar, emphasising the fairness of her hair and the faint tinge of apricot that underlay her tan. Because of her colouring she seldom wore blue, but tonight the green flecks in the wide-set amber eyes seemed to catch and hold the brilliance of the azure. It was a pity she possessed no eye make-up, went through her mind, but the lipstick was her own shade and the compact had provided a smooth powdered skin.

Turning round in a quick pirouette, the pleats flying about her legs, she caught up the bag with which she had arrived, and drawing breath like a swimmer does before a deep dive, went out to meet whatever the man had in store for her.

He was not waiting for her at the front door but was standing on the balcony gazing out over the ocean. Her entrance to the living room made no sound on the thick carpet, but he must somehow have sensed that she was there, because he turned at once and came through the wide glass doors, shutting and locking them, she noticed.

He walked towards her, no amusement showed on his countenance this time. He smiled formally as he said, 'Will you spit at me if I say, instead of, "and not very nice, too" that you look charming?'

Unable to prevent it, Christina felt the flush of colour that stained her cheeks at the compliment, and looked at this man who, from what his uncle had implied, had more than his pick of beautiful women. As his expression showed only the sincerity of his words, she smiled suddenly directly at him—the first time she had ever done so—and said, 'Thank you. I'm glad you feel your money was well spent.'

These words did bring a grin to his face, but he only moved around her and unlocked the door. In silence they crossed the foyer; in silence also they stood as the lift plummeted down. But as he handed her into the Jaguar, he smiled and said interrogatively, an eyebrow climbing, 'I don't have to lock the door from the dashboard tonight, I take it?' And again the colour ran bright upon her cheeks, but she returned no answer.

Through the brilliantly lighted streets of this heart of the Gold Coast they drove, neon lights flashing everywhere, noise and laughter echoing through the open windows. Apparently the driver had decided they would inhale fresh air instead of air-conditioning. Driving now through only sparsely lighted streets, they were gradually beginning to climb the heights behind the city. Lying back in her seat, Christina allowed the breeze to cool her hot cheeks and from under her lashes, glanced sideways at that indolently relaxed figure behind the wheel.

He might have said, 'You look charming,' about her, but *he* looked devastating—fawn slacks, tailored to fit lean hips and flat waist, the thinnest cashmere fashioning a casual rolled-top sweater, the pristine whiteness of which made the bronzed tan of his skin seem so much darker. It also made that incredible hair look as white as itself in the faint light reflected back at them from the dashboard.

Then they were turning from the road on to a circular gravelled driveway and inching forward had pulled into a parking lot. Ashley slipped from behind the wheel and opened her door. As she stepped out in her turn, waiting as her companion closed and locked the Jaguar, Christina glanced back the way they had come. Beneath, the occasional light began halfway down the foothills, becoming more plentiful as the street lights and houses appeared, then further still the glare of Surfers Paradise sent its neon brilliance to colour the sky above in orange flame.

Fingers settled upon her arm to guide her into the restaurant, and the tingle of shock rocked through her entire system. Before, they had only stood together; this was different, this closeness of being actually held. She walked beside him because she had to, and tried to present an outward calmness once they entered the lighted interior.

There, the hold on her arm dropping, her own hand went up to clasp itself around the place which still held the vividness of his close-held fingers. Her companion was being greeted by a waiter who was saying, 'You didn't ring, Mr Carlton, your particular table has been reserved, but,' the man smiled at them both as he continued, 'things can be arranged,' and walked them between diners.

Christina saw him withdraw a Reserved sign from a table situated before open space. No windows hemmed in this dining room; a waist-high wall was the only bulwark against the outside world. She sat in the chair which was being pulled out for her, then saw that another waiter had materialised beside her companion. He was holding out the largest menu she had ever seen. Ashley looked from this person to Christina and his eyebrows climbed. 'I think no drinks for the present, Steven. I'll need to consult my guest's tastes first; I don't actually know them all yet.' They smiled at one another as men do, in complete understanding.

'Now,' giving his attention to the first waiter he took his menu, 'what would you like to eat, Christina?' and made to hand across the large black cardboard folder.

He received a shake of the head and she told him a little shyly, 'I eat mostly anything. . . .' With the waiter standing there beside them she couldn't bring herself to say Mr Carlton, so contented herself with not actually addressing him.

Back and forth the talk went between the two men, and then the folder was closed and their servitor departed. 'I've ordered seafood, Christina. Will you enjoy that?'

She nodded her head. The man across from her grinned, but let it pass, and continued, 'We're having prawn cocktails to start with, but I'll have you know that the kind they serve here are as much like the ordinary prawn cocktail as chalk is to cheese. This restaurant is famous for its cuisine, especially for its seafood.' He settled back to allow the waiter to set before him the crystal container set in its bowl of crushed ice.

'Do you like it?' she was asked after the first forkful, and glancing across at him, she smiled and nodded. However, suddenly she wasn't smiling or nodding. Ashley had reached out a hand placing it over hers which had been lying on the table beside her plate. Her other hand holding the fork went still and her gaze remained downcast upon her food.

'Christina?' She made no move to look up or answer. He said again, 'Christina. . . .' and as she raised her

glance, said 'I know that whatever is worrying you
seems as large as a mountain, but I really can help you.
Money may not solve all problems, but it can help . . .
and influence can help a great deal more. So. . . .'

Transfixed, she gazed at him, then shook her head. 'No
. . . I mean . . . I mean it might not be as bad as I thought. I
haven't seen. . . .' The shaking voice ceased. She couldn't
tell him she hadn't seen any headlines which would
certainly have been carried by the newspapers if what she
feared had eventuated. She couldn't tell him . . . and she
vowed then and there that she would make herself ring the
office the next day and not only ring the house as she had
been doing. She could give another name, she. . . .
Frightened again, she shook her head.

'Please,' she entreated, 'let's not think of it now. I'd
just like to enjoy tonight. It's lovely here.' She threw
out her unclasped hand in a throwaway gesture at the
colourful scene surrounding them, to the openness
beyond. And unexpectedly, the hand over her hand
departed and she could breathe again. A finger was
lifted and the wine waiter was with them.

'Do you drink wine, Christina?' and at her shake of
the head Ashley remarked, laughing, 'I do realise that
you can make your head do most of your talking, but
sometimes . . . just sometimes, I'd like to have your
answer in words. I've never known anyone who could
make a shake of the head mean so emphatic a No, or a
nod of the head say Yes, you would like it very much—
or alternately, that Yes, that's all right, but you
couldn't care less. Now, Christina, do you drink wine?'

Automatically, she went to shake her head, then said
softly, 'I've had it served to me, but I don't like it at all.'

'Have you tried champagne?'

Again she went to nod, then made herself say, 'I have
drunk it a couple of times—at a wedding, and at a
twenty-first birthday party. I didn't dislike it.'

'Well, that's a beginning.' He turned to the man
standing beside him and gave an order.

CHAPTER FIVE

FROM then on he talked quietly to her about the coast, and as the first course was being removed, about food and drink, just casual subjects. Then as the main course was being set before them, he told her, 'It's crab Mornay, and like the prawns, a speciality of this place. I often have it when I dine here, and I always think the salad they serve with it is the best I've tasted anywhere,' he was informing her as dishes were placed before them.

At his words, Christina glanced at her side salad, and hesitantly brought a forkful to her mouth. Blindingly, without knowing she was doing it, she smiled at him as the flavour of the vegetables permeated. 'It's unlike any salad I've ever had before,' she told him, taking up another forkful of the utterly strange-tasting herbs.

'Hey!' he admonished her. 'Eat some of your crab too, they are supposed to go together.'

So she pushed her fork down through the hard cheese-topped crust, and like the salad, found it an altogether different experience. She ate slowly and answered when Ashley spoke, then she noticed a party of two couples glance over at her companion and wave—and saw, too, that though he waved back smilingly, he had turned fully away, presenting only a shoulder to the new arrivals.

'Do you realise, Christina, that I know nothing of your likes and dislikes? Do you play tennis, ride horses, swim, read books, or dance, or even cook?' he was asking.

Replying to such innocuous questions, Christina smiled and answered normally. 'I don't play tennis, or at least, not now. I did of course play sometimes at school, and I've never ridden a horse. I do swim.' Here,

suddenly, her smile widened and she said as she had
done about her typewriting, 'I swim quite well, actually
... and what else? Oh, yes, I love reading ... and I
adore dancing.' She stopped speaking as the waiter
began to open a gold-foiled bottle. The cork flew off
with a bang and foaming liquid was being poured for
Ashley to taste. Then it was her glass being filled and
the waiter had departed.

Ashley raised his glass and said, 'To a closer
acquaintance, Christina.'

Picking up the long-stemmed crystal, she only
nodded and raised it to her lips. She drank properly
because he had troubled to find something she might
like, and felt the bubbles tingle inside her mouth and
down her throat.

'Good girl,' said Ashley. 'Drink it with your dinner.
One glass of champagne won't hurt you. Now, I'm
pleased you like swimming, as I do too. As for dancing,
even if you might think I'm so old as to be past it, I
quite enjoy that. So we'll have to go dancing together
some time.'

Startled eyes looked up quickly and she said before
she could stop herself, 'Don't be silly!'

'Now, what do those words mean—that you agree
that I'm too old to dance, or that you don't want to go
dancing with me?'

'Of course I don't mean you're too old to dance ...
heavens, someone like you! I meant I couldn't go
dancing with you!'

'Why?'

Christina took a big gulp of champagne as the one
word came at her, and replied herself with one word.

'Because. . . .'

'Because what?'

'Look, Mr Carlton. . . .' she began, and was stopped
abruptly, as this time his voice came clipped, curt.

'I can say in your words, Christina, don't be silly,
only I could use more emphatic language about your

Mr Carltoning me. I told you my name the first time I met you—which, I might add, is more than you did. And if you can't remember it, I can tell you what it is.'

'I don't need to be told,' and this time it was her voice that carried tartness. 'How could I not know, when Han says Mr Ashley a dozen times a day? It's just that I can't. . . .'

'But you can try, can't you? Finish up that glass of wine and see if that loosens your tongue.'

Angrily, she drank her glass empty, and said defiantly, 'There, it makes no difference!' and then felt the warmth of the quickly drunk wine creep through her. She looked at him directly and said, 'Very well. Thank you, Ashley, for bringing me here for dinner. I've enjoyed it immensely!'

Across from her, his eyes were suddenly hooded, then abruptly the lids flew up and he was laughing at her. 'When you do do something, Christina, you do it quite handsomely. Now, about this going dancing.' He dropped the sentence casually while forking up some food. 'Wouldn't you like to dance with me?'

The colour didn't rush up into her face; it receded, and for a moment the sounds in the restaurant, the people about her disappeared, and she could neither move nor speak. She had suddenly seen herself dancing with Ashley . . . being held by Ashley. . . . She shook her head, and the night returned to focus. She said, her voice low, 'You don't like me to tell you not to be silly, but that suggestion is. You move in a different world from the one I do. You're used to your own kind of people—sophisticated, clever, and, when they're women, beautiful,' she added defiantly, hearing the echo of his uncle's voice.

'Do you ever look in a mirror, Christina?' Pleasantly, softly, the reply to her emphatic words came.

A frown furrowed the smooth brows, puzzlement showing in her eyes at this abrupt change of subject. Then, as enlightment came, she shook her head decisively. 'Yes,' she answered, 'I look in mirrors, and I see that I'm averagely attractive. However, I don't possess that sheen of high gloss, that imprint of beauty that comes with having been born that way, and, in most cases, of knowing it, and acting accordingly.'

'Then I'll tell you something, Christina.' Suddenly, one eyebrow was raised and his eyes glinted with an emotion she couldn't define as he continued. But she did notice that that peculiar slur had come again to colour his tone—the one he got after speaking with Han, or when he was angry. He didn't seem angry now, though. 'I'll tell you something,' he repeated, 'that when you begin to look at men with those speaking eyes of yours, you'll have them more than turn for a second look. They'll want to get close enough to find out what lies behind them, and I'll have you understand that I know what I'm talking about. A dozen years of experience vouches for that. So we're back to where we started. Would you like to come dancing with me some time?'

Her plate empty, thankfully she pushed it away, unwilling to answer. Ashley must have sent out some sort of signal, because a waiter was by the table, refilling his glass, and pouring only a small portion of the bubbling liquid into hers, removing used dishes, and enquiring about dessert from a trolley pulled alongside.

'No,' she answered to both enquiring faces, and then to Ashley himself, 'I really couldn't. I've eaten enough,' then glancing up at the waiter, she told him, 'The food was delicious, and all that looks delicious too,' she gestured to the laden cart beside them, 'but maybe next time,' she finished—and didn't see the sudden smile flash across her companion's features at her unconscious use of those last few words.

'Then some coffee, I think,' was all he said. But again came that gesture of one raised eyebrow that she was beginning to know, as he asked, 'I expect you won't have a brandy with it,' and laughed out loud as she began to shake her head.

'A cognac,' he ordered, 'and two coffees. White or black?' he asked across to her.

Instead of giving a definite answer, some imp of mischief caused her to reply, 'Oh, like sour dinner wine, I haven't graduated to black coffee yet. I'll have mine with dollops of cream floating on top!'

For the second time that night Ashley laughed at her outright, but as the waiter was turning away he lifted a long brown finger and when the man bent to listen, he spoke softly into his ear.

Apparently with nothing more to say for the time being, he then sat indolently, gazing out at the darkness beyond, drinking his champagne. Christina raised her own glass too, but only sipped as she gazed round the brightly lighted room, at the diners intent on enjoying themselves. And with relief she saw that though evening dresses predominated, there were also short cocktail frocks, and even ordinary, though expensive, afternoon wear. She heaved a sigh of relief. After seeing where they were dining, she had wondered.

Coffee was being set before them—a small cup in front of Ashley set beside a large balloon glass which held only a small amount of glinting amber liquid; a larger container before herself, almost a tea-cup, she reflected. She picked up the tiny silver coffee spoon and stirred the heavy cream, floating it round and round.

As the brandy glass was lifted and drunk from, Christina raised her own cup. She swallowed, then set it down again, saying.

'What's in it?'

'My dear Christina, surely you've graduated to creamed coffee?' Blandness wasn't the word for the tone in which he spoke. 'Don't you like it?'

It was with honesty that she replied, not as she had about the champagne, 'Yes, I do like it—very much!'

'It's called Roman coffee, and has a liqueur called

Galliano added. And you actually like it!' he laughed at her, sounding pleased, then he raised his balloon glass to her in a toast.

They sat companionably finishing the coffee, then as she pushed back her empty cup, he upended his own, and said, 'Time to go. You have to begin your new job tomorrow, don't forget. Are you worried about starting it?'

Automatically Christina began to shake her head, then reading the smile beginning to form upon his lips, said instead, 'No. Because it's not an important job. I'll just do as I'm told, and I *can* type very well if I'm given any to do. . . .' Then as he raised a hand to the waiter for his bill, she thought, I'm not worried, because I probably won't be there long enough.

Her companion was placing notes on a tray handed to him. Brushing away some murmured words, he was rising to pull Christina's chair out, and it was with a grin that he added, 'Count yourself lucky that it was you serving me tonight, because, for me, tonight has been all I was hoping it to be, so I'm feeling generous.' Christina didn't understand what he was alluding to, but apparently the waiter did. He raised a hand and said only, 'Okay—thanks.'

Out in the night again, Christina shook her head. She felt funny, keyed-up, and wondered if it was what she had drunk. But that fact might only have added to this feeling. It was the man beside her who was the main reason; not a glass and a half of champagne drunk with a meal.

The drive back home was conducted in almost total silence, and she lay back, as she had done on the outward journey, gazing at the profile presented to her; not as she had done then, surreptitiously, but openly. In the faint light reflected from the dashboard, it appeared carved from bronze. Brilliant saffron, as lights from oncoming cars outlined it, purple ebony as the darkness closed in again.

It wasn't late, and they drove back through crowded streets once again before turning off to their own unit. In the foyer, waiting for Ashley to unlock the door, Christina glanced around this place which was becoming so familiar. Inside, the long room was hushed, quiet, empty; a small, dim night light burning on an ivory side table against the wall. The man turned them towards the corridor, and at his guest's room, said casually, pleasantly, 'Goodnight, Christina. Thank you for giving me such an enjoyable evening.'

She made no attempt to open the door, but just stood there, unable to make herself do so. An arm reached out behind her and thrust it wide, switching on the light as it did so.

'Go to bed, Christina,' came the words, and the voice had suddenly lost its casualness. And still she didn't move, but stood close against him.

'Christina!' and at no reply forthcoming, her name came again. 'Christina . . .?'

Then she did look up, directly into his gaze. Standing apart, he didn't touch her, but his head came down and his lips were on hers, lightly, as gently as a butterfly might alight. The girl's eyes closed, and it was her body that arched to meet his, her curves that melted into the hard body standing away from her. For a long second the two unmoving bodies remained as if caught and held in frozen immobility. Then a hand had come to spreadeagle against her back and she was pulled so close that the two figures became one entity.

His lips weren't gently caressing now; they were moving on the ones lifted so willingly, bringing unknown desires to the girl in his arms. Then they had departed, but not lifting, they were finding their way along cheek and throat to send shivers of shock through an unawakened body. If the man realised that, he didn't stop his deliberate, his experienced embrace— or the caresses that were leaving on their journey a trail of fire that spread molten throughout her entire system.

Finally, those searching lips came to where they desired, ending in the cleft which the white sailor collar exposed.

Her head thrown back against the arm supporting it, hair hanging long and shining upon the white sweater, eyes closed, Christina lay there, feeling those lips, needing to respond and not knowing how, yet desiring them to go on and on. . . .

However, it was Ashley's head that jerked suddenly upright, and with a hand at the nape of her neck, brought hers level as well. 'Christina . . .?' It was a whisper and she knew somewhere deep inside that it was a question, and that he might go, leave her. . . . She raised both hands to clasp behind his neck and pressed even closer against him.

This time, when his kisses resumed, she gave as much of herself as she knew how . . . and felt the entire atmosphere around their two clinging forms disintegrate. This . . . this was a different lovemaking; a demand that wanted everything; caresses that were leading up to complete fulfilment. She felt the shudder that encompassed her whole body as the hand at her back pulled her deliberately into the proximity of his own; the lips begin to lose their searching quality and settle into slow heartbreaking caresses that were drawing the soul from her.

Responding now, thinking of nothing but the man holding her, the emotions, the desires he was engendering—Christina felt the world crash about her as the hand abruptly left her back and two hands went up to prize apart her own clasped so tightly about his neck.

'No . . .!' the word exploded into the hushed quietness of the space around them, then again, still loudly, but less violently. 'No . . . Christina,' and the hands gripping her wrists tightened cruelly. 'No,' he repeated for the third time, and added, 'Go to bed, Christina.'

Before he could release that taut grip about her wrists, she shook her head, endeavouring to sway towards him—and was held back. 'No,' he said again. 'I don't know how I started this. I had no intention of doing so. . . .'

'But I don't care. . . .' Christina was beginning, and was surprised at the sound of her voice, slurred, unsteady, desire-laden. 'I don't care. . . .' she made herself repeat, while the grip on her arms tightened even further.

'But I do.' His voice had lost any caressing tone it might have held, even if it did show strain. 'I bloody care . . . and you, Christina, just don't realise what the result of all this could be. I do. This sort of scene should never have started.' And again he held her away as she tried to sway into him.

Overriding the words she was beginning, he told her, 'I'm not starting it again. I can understand—well, partly—your wishes now, but tomorrow is another day. And, allow me to inform you, all tomorrows bring their own reckonings, so you go to bed now—and by yourself.'

And as she still didn't move, but just stood gazing at him, the expression in the green-flecked amber eyes showing openly, his hand did return to spreadeagle along her body; not to bring her melting into his embrace, however, but to turn her round. And it was with almost a push that he sent her in through the lighted doorway, the other hand reaching out to shut the door.

Christina remained where she had ended up, rigid, her metabolism still back there with him in the corridor. No sound penetrated from it of course. The carpet was too thick.

She didn't want to go to bed . . . she didn't want to. . . . And she wondered suddenly what Ashley would say, or do, if she walked down the hallway and knocked at his door . . . and. . . . Unexpectedly, the enormity of what she was thinking brought her out of her daze. God! Shuddering, she drew breath, and like a blind person, walked falteringly towards the bathroom.

Stepping out of her clothes, she allowed them to fall to the floor, then she stood under the streaming water. Her face also she held up to it, thinking to wash away all signs of the previous seconds—vowing never again to give him the option of repudiating any advance of hers. And deciding also that she would be departing in the morning, and that most likely ... no, most probably now ... Ashley would be more than willing to let her go.

Out, dried, the towel wrapped sarong-fashion around her, still hazy, but able to think a little more clearly, she picked up her discarded clothes and went into the bedroom. Automatically smoothing the dress on to a hanger, she patted it into place and said softly, 'There! I'll possibly never wear you again, but I'll always keep you to remind me of tonight.' The soft voice faltered and Christina turned swiftly away, taking up the nightdress Han had placed on the pillow when he had come to check the room for the night. Donning it, she went over to the window, touching the button to allow the curtains to swish apart.

Feeling less like sleep than she had ever done, she leant her forehead against the cool glass. Far below, cars were still rushing in two streams of headlights to their destinations and farther away to the back of the esplanade the lights of the main drag were flaring their illumination to the sky. But up here no sound penetrated.

Inexperienced as she was, Christina was still nearly through her teens and had been going out socially for the last year. She knew that men could take love—or sex, she amended—in their stride; and certainly she knew that they were willing to take what was freely offered ... and she *had* offered. It had been her fault, she knew absolutely, that that scene in the corridor outside her bedroom had taken place. But Ashley Carlton probably had enough women to pick and choose from ... beautiful, experienced women, she had

no doubt. He had no need for what he believed was a
waif in trouble to satisfy his urges. But ... but ... he
hadn't sounded as if he didn't want her when he had so
abruptly stopped that passion-laden interlude. She
wished she knew ... and realised she didn't ... the
whys and wherefores of it. She sighed, and continued
leaning there, knowing she didn't want to go to bed,
that she wouldn't sleep if she did; supine against the
cool window, all energy gone.

She did hear the knock upon her door, however, and
startled, turned huge eyes towards it. When she didn't
answer the knock came again, firmly; no tentative tap,
this, and without waiting for a summons, the door
opened.

Framed in the aperture stood Ashley, with a glass in
his hand. He said, 'Get into bed, Christina.'

Gazing back at him, still wearing the clothes he had
worn to take her out; that incredibly fair hair glinting
yellow under the overhead light; the face beneath it
appearing almost black in contrast, she only shook her
head, then remembering, said, 'I don't want to. I won't
sleep.'

'Hell!' She heard the almost whispered expletive from
across the space separating them. '*You* won't sleep?
How do you imagine *I'll* manage?' Then he said
again, 'Get into bed, Christina. I've brought you some
of Han's brew, but unlike he did, I'm telling you. It
won't hurt you, and you've gone through a great deal
of distress these last few days.'

Still not venturing further into the room, he gestured
again towards the bed, and as she went to it and pulled
the turned-back covers up to her breasts, he walked
across to hand her the glass. He held it by the top, she
noticed, so that his fingers wouldn't touch hers. He
needn't worry, she thought bitterly. She wouldn't throw
herself at him again.

Holding it because she must, not wanting to drink the
doctored Ovaltine, she kept her gaze down, feeling his

presence towering above her. Then three words were uttered. 'Drink it up!'

She drank it up, and the glass was taken from her hand, the looming presence departing. Ashley stood at the door with his hand on the switch and told her gently, 'Goodnight, Christina. Sleep well.' The light flashed off and he was gone.

She lay there watching the faint illumination which was spilling in through the uncurtained windows, thinking of him, wondering if he would also be taking some of what he called Han's brew. Somehow she didn't think so. Still, he had sounded kind when he had come; not at all as if he was disgusted by her behaviour ... her.... Her eyelids began to droop as more even breathing took over.

CHAPTER SIX

Next morning, not knowing what else to do, going along with the tide, Christina dressed in the skirt and lemon blouse, slipping her feet into the heeled sandals she had worn last night ... last night; her mind shied away from anything to do with that period of time. So, using her compact and lipstick, head held high, she opened her door. The apartment seemed quiet, empty. Her watch said eight o'clock—almost time to start for any working office.

Down the big living room and under the arch into the kitchen she went. Han was there, sitting at the table in the breakfast nook. He was reading the morning paper. He jumped up as he became aware of her, offering her his usual kindly good morning.

'Your breakfast is ready, Miss Christina,' he said. 'Sit while I get it—oh, and there is a note from Mr Ashley. He had to leave early.'

'Yes, I'll bet he did,' muttered the girl as she took her seat and picked up the frosted glass of orange juice. It was an easy way of opting out. Well, she didn't care; she would manage, she told herself defiantly. She sat sipping the yellow liquid and stared at the envelope propped against the sugar basin in front of her.

Unwilling to see the contents which would provide the knowledge that she wouldn't be seeing him again, it was with reluctance that she reached out and gingerly picked up the missive.

It was a plain linen envelope with her first name scrawled right across it in bold black writing, with a straight slash of the pen underlining it.

Folding back the unsealed flap, she withdrew the folded sheet. He hadn't even begun with her name, she thought dismally, probably thinking that having scrawled it across the envelope was enough introduction. It started,

'I've been called away urgently. This is to tell you that the interlude of last night makes no difference to our situation. That if you have any idea of leaving, of disappearing, you'd better have second thoughts. I meant what I said in the beginning—believe me, you wouldn't care for the consequences! Han will drive you to the mill and will call for you at four-thirty when you finish. I'll see you this evening.

Ashley.'

'Well . . .!' indignantly, the drawn-out word came. Talk about arrogant, conceited, overbearing . . .! Her thoughts ran out of adjectives. But underneath them all was a small, secret fire, of a kind of happiness. She wasn't to leave here. She would be seeing Ashley again—and whatever the reason was, why he was determined she was to stay here, she didn't care. She didn't see the smile of satisfaction creeping over the bland, almost always inscrutable face of Han, as he watched her reading the note.

She did hear him say, 'Drink your orange juice, Miss Christina. Your breakfast is ready.' Quickly she put the liquid to her lips and gulped, coughing as too much went down too quickly.

The glass was whisked from her hand, and a plate of bacon and eggs slipped into its place. Still feeling the result of that curt, arrogant letter, Christina glanced down at it with distaste, feeling the nerves beneath her diaphragm reject it. But Han was standing beside her, so she picked up the cutlery and slowly began to eat— and found it went down quite easily. She also found, after drinking the tea Han poured, that the dull throb behind her eyes with which she had awakened was gradually disappearing.

That rotten champagne, and that rotten Italian stuff

flavouring her coffee were responsible, she told herself.
Then, thinking of the later happenings of the night, she
decided viciously, that they could be the cause of her
uninhibited behaviour too. . . .

'It's a quarter past eight, Miss Christina. You should
be at the mill in half an hour. Are you nearly finished?'
Han's quiet voice broke in on the miserable reflections,
so with a push her chair went back and she rose from
the table. Then with an abrupt turn that sent the severe
skirt twisting about her legs, she swung back to snatch
up the envelope from the table.

She held it in fingers conscious of it all the way to her
room, and instead of dropping it on to the dressing
table, placed it carefully in the small shoulder bag.
Teeth brushed, lipstick applied carefully to meet her
fellow workers in a new job, in two minutes she had
joined Han who was waiting with the door open.

At the mill he pulled in to the side, away from the
men working in the so differently busy area from what
it had been on Sunday when Ashley . . . Ashley . . . had
brought her. She got herself out, sent a flippant wave to
her driver, then moved round to the front entrance of
the office. She walked through the wide doors and as
she did so saw beyond them the Holden departing
coastwards.

Inside, she saw beyond a long polished counter a
large open space with a couple of big desks, the usual
impedimenta of a busy office, and two girls conferring.
One of them glanced round as the new arrival entered,
then moved towards her. She was beginning to speak
when Christina pre-empted her a trifle breathlessly.

'Hi, there. I'm Christina Seaton,' and before she
could continue, she answered with a smile, even if there
was a faintly surprised look in the eyes looking her
over, taking in the smooth pageboy bob, the severe skirt
and cool lemon blouse, the young pretty face which
spoke in such an assured voice.

'Yes, do come in.' The girl was lifting a flap in the

counter as she spoke, then she continued, 'I'm Jenny Condon, and this is Julia Sydney. I'm afraid you're going to find us all at sixes and sevens. The clerk whose place I'm taking left on Friday, leaving a mass of work not even started. I'm moving up a grade, and Julia is promoted to my old job. We were expecting a junior office girl. Have you worked before? Actually,' here she smiled as she again looked Christina over, 'you don't look like a junior office girl!'

'Well, no, I'm probably not. I'm not experienced. But I have been studying in a secretarial college, so if you'll give me some work we'll see how I manage.'

'There's all Mr Fenton's dictated letters from Friday to begin with,' the girl called Jenny was beginning, then she stopped suddenly as she caught the expression on Christina's face. 'What is it?'

'I'm sorry, I don't read—or take—shorthand,' said Christina.

'Oh!'

The younger girl, Julia, broke in. 'Look, Jenny, I can do the letters off the shorthand notes if . . . Christina can type. Can you?' she asked, and there was a hopeful look on her face. 'There's a whole stack of government forms which would have been Betty's job until all this upset and I don't know how I'll manage them. I don't understand a lot of the names of timber and trees, and there are things I've never heard of. And they are all for government files and have to be done meticulously. I'd *much* rather do letters and invoices. . . .' her words trailed off and she gazed at the new girl.

'No, Julia, you'll have to manage. I'll be here to help you with them as much as I can. We can't give them to a junior. You know how important they are.'

'I can type. Quite well!' Broke in Christina, and then remembered suddenly when and where she had used those same words before. 'Show me one of these forms and we'll see how I get on.'

Only too happy to comply with this suggestion, Julia

moved to one of the desks and lifted out a huge bundle of folders, dumping them beside an electric typewriter on the second desk.

Hanging her bag over the chair back, Christina looked the typewriter over, nodded familiarity with it and took up just one sheet of paper. Opening the top folder, she scanned its contents and began to type. The click-clack of expert typing filled the air about them as the two girls still stood beside her, watching. A half page Christina typed, then ripped it out, handing it to the older woman.

It was both the girls who looked it over, and then Jenny said. 'Thank heavens. Okay, go and do those letters, Julia. I'll show Christina how to do these in triplicate, and then I'll get in and try to put some order into Mr Fenton's office.'

Carefully, exactly, the first three sheets and carbons were inserted, and, slowly at first, feeling her way, not wanting to make mistakes, she began. Then as her confidence grew, so too, did the speed of her work, and it was with surprise that she glanced up when Julia touched her on the shoulder.

'Morning tea time, Christina. It used to be my job, it's yours now. But I'll do it this morning if you like, while you get on with those,' she flicked a finger at the big heap of folders still waiting to be completed, then glanced admiringly as well as gratefully at the ones already finished.

'No.' Pushing back her chair, Christina looked up. 'I'll make the tea. Just show me where the paraphernalia is, and I'll find my way around it.' If she could find her way around the complexities of Han's kitchen, she decided that making simple office morning tea would be a breeze. And so it turned out to be. There was a teapot for the girls and three beakers, and a tray for Mr Fenton to be taken into an office devoid of his presence at the moment. She made the tea, asked preferences and poured. She had wondered why Han had given her what looked like a small attaché case with no handle this morning, as he said something about there being no canteen. She had thought he was just being kind, as he always was to her, and providing a few non-essentials.

As the two girls delved into their own carryalls for something to eat with their tea, Christina unclasped the lid of her receptacle. It disclosed some of Han's thinly cut sandwiches, two brown things of what looked like flaky pastry, and two large peaches. 'Good heavens!' she muttered. 'What will these girls think?' and then thought herself that Han must have made it his business to find out where the staff ate, and where they got their supplies. She took out one of the brown things and bit into it. Like everything in the food line that she associated with Han, it was delicious ... unknown, but delicious. It tasted of honey and nuts, and ... she gave up trying to identify flavours, and sat with her tea, listening to the gossip going on between the two girls, pleased that she had more than satisfied Jenny with her work, and, most of all, that that damned Ashley Carlton would find out that as he had sent her, she had proved herself quite competent.

The day wore on, the statistics for the government going downwards, even if the ordinary day-to-day mill work was piling up while that was being accomplished. Jenny had said that they should have been in two weeks ago, that the senior girl had left everything in a mess. She had added, 'I'm going to get things up to date, and keep them there, now I've got the senior job. Just watch me!'

Christina believed her, scenting how thrilled she was that the unexpected upset had allowed her to come by a position which normally she would have to wait some years for.

At twenty-past four she came through the glass partition that screened the manager's office which had been kept open today to allow her to oversee them. She said now, 'Okay, cover your typewriters, and put your folders and work away. Knocking off time!'

'I'll just finish this. . . .' Christina was beginning, but was told a little sharply,

'No, you won't, Christina. We have to walk down to catch a bus into town and it's the only one that comes along for over an hour, so now is finishing time.'

Julia had already covered her typewriter and retrieved a handbag from out of her desk, so Christina did the same, stacking the completed work into a deep drawer. 'They should be finished tomorrow,' she told Jenny. 'I expect that will please you.'

'Too right,' answered Jenny. 'And we won't be so pressed then, so you'll be able to take it a little easier.'

'You're not catching the bus, Christina?' asked Julia, as they walked outside, and of necessity, she replied,

'No, not today. I'm being called for. My Aunt Beth to whom I was sent for a visit felt that until I'd found my feet—her words, not mine—I should be brought and taken home. It's just for a few days.' The unblushing lie came out straight-faced.

She was vouchsafed a wave and they were hurrying off. In her turn, Christina made her way to where Han was waiting, knowing that she had meant to ring today to try definitely to find out where she stood. She had been unable to, with not a free minute near a telephone to ring unheard. Maybe tomorrow. . . .

Leaning back on the fender of the station wagon, Han straightened and opened the door. She returned his smile, but it was in silence that the first part of the journey was accomplished, the girl's thoughts focusing on the dilemma she was in.

'How did the day go, Miss Christina? Did you manage all right?' Han's voice broke into the silence as they cruised slowly along.

She turned sideways looking at him and said, 'Oh yes, Han. I managed very well. In fact, I think I got them out of a difficulty. But how I'll go on ordinary office work remains to be seen,' and with her glance still on the saffron, impassive face, she asked in her turn, 'And how did your day go, Han?'

For the briefest moment his glance left the road in front of him, and he too, smiled. 'I returned to the penthouse after dropping you because Tuesday morning is the day the cleaners come in. They do windows and floors, and tiles, that sort of thing—all the jobs associated with hard labour, because they have the machinery for it.'

'Oh. . . . I expected that place never got dirty. It seems to be always immaculate.'

In his turn, Han interrupted, and his silent laugh was there. 'I'm afraid it wouldn't stay immaculate if it wasn't cleaned. I manage the rest, but the heavy work is done once a week by a crew of service cleaners. When they had gone I went to the restaurant.'

'Oh, do you work elsewhere, Han?' Surprise coloured Christina's voice. She would never have thought it.

'Well, yes and no. I own the restaurant, but some of my countrymen run it. But when Mr Ashley has no need of me I go and help, or I go home. I have a wife and daughter, you know.'

'No . . . no, I didn't know.' Christina's voice went high in absolute surprise. 'How lovely, Han! And how old is your daughter?'

'She is two. You won't know, Miss Christina, that I helped . . . that I was in Vietnam with Mr Ashley. I was seventeen when I first met him, and he was twenty. He kept a flat in Saigon for when he was on leave. That was when he began to talk our . . . my . . . language.' Unexpectedly, funnily, Han was stumbling on this explanation, but nevertheless, continued. 'He got so good that the Army used him . . . and me.

'Then when he came home I came with him. He knew. . . . He had had contact with another family over there and nominated them for Australia. It took four years, though. But when they did get here I married one of the daughters. So with the salary I had saved and Mr Ashley's guarantee, I bought the restaurant.' Here, Han laughed. 'You've no idea what it was like—run-down, not in the best district. But it is spick and span now, and doing very well, thank you. Also, we are happy, and so thankful to be here.'

'I simply hadn't realised, Han. I thought there were only the two of you. You must be away from your wife a lot. Doesn't she mind?'

There was more than a smile in the voice answering. 'No, of course she doesn't mind. Even if I wasn't with her either at home or at the restaurant quite a lot—which I am, as Mr Ashley is often away, I owe him, we all owe him, our lives out here. He comes first with us all. He is a wonderful man, Miss Christina!'

The girl beside him kept silent. What could she say? As far as she was concerned he was a wonderful man too . . . but she wasn't Han. And he had walked away and left her last night . . . last night. . . . She shook her head to clear it. Would he be at home this evening, and how would he treat her? She was soon to know. Han was running the car into the underground car park.

Inside the big room her glance went searching. Ashley was out on the balcony. Although evening shadows were stretching ebony across the buildings, he was still outlined in the sunshine at this height. He turned as they entered and came down the long room with that lithe lion's-prowl walk that she remembered, only now, it seemed to her standing there, silent, trying to calm her nerves to meet his gaze, that that easy, indolent movement was more pronounced.

His expression carried only pleasant casualness. 'Hi there. How did the first day's work go?' he asked.

She went to nod her head, but remembering, said, 'I think it went fairly well. I typed statistics for some government department which seems to want them in a hurry. They're screaming about overdue estimates or something. . . .'

'Good God,' she was interrupted, 'don't tell me you
did those! I've been getting bombarded at head office
about them. It appears I've sent a goldmine up to that
mill. Did you really do those intricate forms by
yourself?' He stopped speaking as her head began to
nod yes. He laughed.

'You deserve a present for doing them. Go and get
into your bikini and we'll have a swim here in the pool.'

Christina went to shake her head, and met his eyes.
They were telling her they wouldn't take no for an
answer. So she turned abruptly away, and in her room,
slipped into her bikini. She looked at the yellow
towelling dress, needing a cover-up in which to go down
to the pool, then shrugged, and went into the bathroom
to catch up one of the huge bath-towels, slinging it
across one shoulder so it fell down at both back and
front. Then, slipping her feet into the beach scuffs she
had worn on arriving at this place, she went out.

Ashley was waiting for her in swimming briefs, and
unexpectedly, like her, he too, had a towel slung across
a shoulder. This one, however, was one of those large,
bright, beautiful beach affairs. He looked her over, then
stood aside for her to go through the door.

His behaviour was perfect, she reflected. He guided
her to the pool, dropped his towel and scuffs on the
grass verge beside the inlaid edge, then dived in.

Because of the dressing on her leg Christina was
thankful that there were only two other people
swimming, a couple at the far end. Ashley's citrine
head, a shade darker now with water dripping from it,
cut through the cerulean depths beneath him, and
placing two hands on the pool-side he swung himself up
to sit beside her. She dived, and they swam together,
then drifted to the edge of the pool to hang on, then
swam again, Ashley never touching her, or being
anything but a companion she had come down to swim
with. Christina began to think she must have dreamed
last night . . . but she knew she hadn't.

'Had enough, Christina?' asked the man in her thoughts, and at her nod, swam to the steps. He waited until she came through the vivid crystal-clear blueness to him, but made no move to help her. He did bend to catch up her towel, handing it across with an outstretched hand.

Upstairs in her own bedroom, she showered and dressed a leg that seemed to be getting much better every time she did it, uncaringly pulled on the yellow slip-on, combed her hair, lipsticked her lips, then she descended kitchenwards.

But it seemed they were not to eat in the kitchen. The dining room lights were on and the polished table set for two at the far end. Voices came from the kitchen, however, and Christina stood there, undecided.

Then they were both coming towards her, Ashley in casual slacks and an open-necked short-sleeved shirt, Han, as always, in immaculate slacks and the starched top he always wore. He carried a tray, and Ashley pulled out one of the chairs for her. Even afterwards, Christina never knew what she had to eat for that meal. She ate what was placed before her, smiling her thanks; answered when Ashley addressed her, and endeavoured to keep her mind, her clamouring nerves, from the very closeness of him. She did notice, however, that while Han poured white wine for Ashley, in her glass of the same crystal he poured ice water.

'We'll have coffee on the balcony, if you would care for that, Christina,' said Ashley at last. And, out there, he carefully settled her into a cushioned patio chair—for all the world as if she were somebody's grandmother, acidly came the reflection to the girl's mind.

Han was joining them, carrying a silver tray which he deposited on a side table. He put coffee, black, and in a large cup, beside Ashley, a balloon glass with the small amount of liquid beside it. The same sized cup for Christina, but with cream added. For himself, he took black coffee, but instead of cognac, a thin liqueur glass was set beside it. They talked, drank their coffee, and watched the scene below, then suddenly something Han said, but that she didn't catch, had Ashley answering in Vietnamese.

If afterwards she couldn't remember anything about the dinner that preceded it, this interlude on the balcony was to be forever etched in her memory. Han laughed, and turned to Christina, explaining, 'I've just told Mr Ashley something a man newly come from my country told me today.'

She smiled at him, natural in his company as she had always been. 'Do you miss your own country, Han?' she asked, and then to the other man, said, 'I know nothing about that war, except that sometimes it's mentioned in the newspapers. I was so young when it occurred. Did you mind being there, Ashley, or like it, or hate it?'

'Both,' replied the man by her side. 'We did have some good times, though, didn't we, Han, the three of us in Saigon while I was on leave?'

As Han began to answer in his own language getting the drift of their conversation by now as it went back and forth, Christina knew he had asked a question, and that it was also in the negative that Ashley had replied. Then Han continued, this time in English, 'Not too good when we were on patrol, Miss Christina. Mud, slush, and leeches . . . and the Viet-Cong in hiding when you were careless enough to let them ambush you.'

'We had Han with us, Christina, against Army regulations, you understand, but weren't we glad of it! Do you remember, Han . . . that snake and that officer. . . .' Han laughed and Ashley grinned; the first time she had seen him do it, naturally, only thinking of amusing happenings. The speech flashed back and forth, now in English, now in Han's language. Christina was enthralled. Laughter would overtake them, and then Christina would be shown the picture, and the way Han told it, she found herself laughing with them. She loved it, and unexpectedly felt a sense of belonging. She might have wondered, when it was mentioned, who had been the third person of the trio that Ashley had mentioned, but then it had faded from her mind.

It was after a small silence had fallen that Han stretched and remarked, 'I'll just clear these away, and then I'm off. I'll be here to get breakfast in the morning, Mr Ashley.'

Ashley raised a lazy agreeing hand as Han rose to begin collecting coffee cups and glasses. Then he said, 'Goodnight, Miss Christina,' and departed. Christina made to rise as well, but subsided as her companion spoke. 'I've got some work to do, but it's only nine-thirty. Would you care to watch the television, Christina. There's a *TV Times* on the set.'

'No, I don't think so, thank you. I might read for a while and then go to bed. I'm a bit tired. I expect working to a set schedule might account for that, as I'm not used to it. But ... Ashley,' she glanced across the space separating them, space that was only illuminated by lights spreading up from below, and a soft gleam from the big living room behind, 'but, Ashley,' she repeated, 'there is really no need for me to stay here now. You've got me a job, and.... and ....' What could she say, what could she tell him except the truth? And she wasn't going to do that. It was too sordid.

'I accept that there's no need, Christina. I'll take you home now if you like. You know that—I've told you so!'

Her glance slid away and she shrugged. But she would, she really would, try to find out where she stood in the morning. The telephone shrilling inside made her jump, literally. She had never got used to Ashley, or Han, disregarding it as they went unconcernedly about their business. It stopped as was usual as the recording machine took over.

'Well, I'll leave you to get on with your work. I'm off to bed. Goodnight.' She was up in one quick movement and as quickly went through the door. There was no

way a repetition of her last night's behaviour was going
to occur. But in an even more swift movement Ashley
had caught her up and was standing before her.

'Christina?' he said. 'Look, I'm not going to say I'm
sorry about last night. I'm not!' And as she went to
hurriedly depart, he caught hold of her arm. 'Listen to
me,' he told her. 'You wouldn't know ... you *wouldn't*
... how much I wanted to make love to you last night,
how much it cost me to walk away. But it wouldn't
have been right. I have my commitments too. So could
you leave things as they are for the time being and we'll
see what our tomorrows bring, eh?'

Christina remained silent. What did he mean? She
knew that with those fingers clasping her arm, sending
needles of tension all through her, what it was she
wanted. But he had said he had commitments. Well, she
wouldn't want to interfere with those. Her head came
up proudly, but as it did, her gaze met his, and at the
expression in it, her bones melted. She didn't care what
he thought of her behaviour ... she didn't care. ... She
swayed towards him.

But it seemed her companion did, his voice carrying a
harshness as he said coldly, 'Cut it out, Christina. This
was to be only a friendly evening. Be fair! I'm not one
of the young teenagers you've been used to knocking
about with. I've been on the town for more years than
I care to remember, and when I start making love, I
expect to do just that. I find I've journeyed beyond
play-acting.'

'Don't worry yourself!' Stung, knowing it had been
herself who had sent the hitherto pleasant evening into
high drama, Christina brought her head up, proudly her
eyes bright. 'It won't happen again, I promise you. I'll
take good care of that ... and while we're on the
subject, I'm leaving here.'

'No, that you're not!' The explosive interruption cut
through her diatribe, and no one could have had the
least doubt about what those words meant.

'Just how are you going to stop me now?' she demanded. 'Ring the mill and tell them I won't be returning? They'll love that when I'm halfway through those rotten statistics!'

'I couldn't care less about the mill. It's merely one of my companies. It exists at *my* pleasure, and if I disrupt its workings, that's the least of my worries. I have my own reasons for wanting you here; and here you stay!'

'Have you, indeed? Of course I'm here at your pleasure, and, in these modern days, rape is a common word, but surely that shouldn't be necessary, seeing that I appear to have known no better than to have met you more than halfway. . . .'

An arm, iron-hard, reached out and she was pulled against him; against a figure that was as rigid as the arm cradling her. There was no melting of curve into curve this time. She was clamped against the inflexibility of a body menacing in its anger.

'What was that word you used?' he was asking from between the whiteness of clenched teeth; and suddenly she was frightened. That slur he sometimes got in his voice had come to match the wicked expression on an abruptly changed face. 'Rape? Well, they tell me a new experience is as good as a holiday, and I haven't had that particular one yet—not even in my war years—so . . . here goes!'

His head came down and lips were upon hers as hard, as demanding, as the arm clamping her to him was. She stood immobile, endeavouring to remain passive under the onslaught. His face came up, and from far back in his throat, he laughed. And as she heard it, a shiver rippled through her.

'Oh, you will, my little girl of mystery,' that slurred voice said. 'You will respond. We've got all night ahead of us and I intend to use it to good purpose.' The arm holding her pulled her even more tightly to him, bringing her body to lie against the whole tensile length of his. But this time his kisses were not hard, gentleness

coming to take over. And there began the heartbreaking
caresses that had shown her how to respond last night.

Her body went slack against the one holding it so
closely, and she felt tears sting her eyelids. She shut
them firmly. Ashley was never going to see her crying,
but they slid out and down her cheeks, and then, as
suddenly as he had done the night before, he set her
away from him. And it was from behind closed lids that
she heard the expletive come . . . and then the following
words. 'Tears, Christina? They do nothing to me. You
more than deserved what you got . . . but this sort of
situation has got to stop! Do you understand me? Now
get out of here!'

But it was he who got out. Christina heard him go
through the dining room, knocking against the table in
his hurry, and then the study door slam. She couldn't
make herself move, caught up in a lethargy over which
she had no control. She sank down on to the carpet and
leaned her head against the side of the sofa—and this
time the tears came openly.

How had that tension-laden scene of a moment ago
happened? she wondered. It had been such a happy
couple of hours previously. But she needn't wonder, she
told herself bitterly. It had been her fault entirely. What
had provoked her to speak so to Ashley? She had never
behaved like this in her life before. But, said some inner
voice, she had never been head over heels, fathoms deep
in love before, either.

She half lay there, head on her arm as the tears fell
and then began to abate, thinking she would have to
make an effort to rise soon and go to her room. She
didn't hear the footsteps that came to her across the
deep carpet; she did feel the touch on her shoulder, and
the voice say, 'Christina. . . .'

She only burrowed her head further into the
cushioned softness of the couch on which she was
leaning, curling deeper into the enfolding arm like a
turtle withdrawing its head from outside interference.

'Christina,' said the soft slurred voice again, then abruptly she was scooped up, and Ashley had dropped into the corner of the sofa, cradling her on his lap.

He pressed the head that was beginning to shake from side to side into his shoulder, and began to stroke the fair hair from the damp face. He didn't speak.

Finally, getting herself under control, Christina said in a small voice, 'I'm sorry, Ashley. It was all my fault!'

'Well, my love,' he said, and she went still. Had he said that? Oh yes, he had said it, but did it mean anything? It had probably been said without thought, and she listened as he continued. 'I won't contradict you on that point. It *was* your fault; but *I* should have known better ... except that you got me so furious. Look, Christina, we'll make a pact. For my own reasons I don't want you to leave here for the time being. How about just going along with the way things are—for a few days, anyway? Will you do that?'

Being where she was, hearing that tone in his voice, she would have done anything, agreed to anything, that he asked. She nodded, and felt the body holding her ripple along its whole length. He was laughing.

With her face in his shoulder, she smiled too, happy that the tension-filled drama of a moment ago was passed, and thought, this is happiness, now, this exact moment—and was content. They lay there, immobile in the silent room. Then Christina felt the body beneath her twist, and, suddenly guilty, she sat up. 'Even if I'm not the world's fattest lady, I'm no lightweight,' she said, and slipped from his knee.

Wryly, a grin appeared on the bronzed face, and he answered, 'If that was my only worry. . . .' and rose to stand beside her. He glanced down. 'If you'd care for some of Han's Ovaltine, we can raid the kitchen. He always swears it's God's gift to sleep. In fact, he uses it on all and every occasion where only the slightest need for it is obvious.'

As they walked companionably towards the lighted

kitchen, Christina asked a little shyly, 'Do you drink it, Ashley?'

'God forbid! I don't say I never have. But it was long ago and far away. I've grown out of it now.'

'What do you drink at bedtime?'

'Well, mostly I have a whisky and soda for a nightcap if I haven't been out. It usually is only one, too. I'm afraid, however, that last night it was more like half a dozen. But tonight,' here, he glanced down at her, white glinting in a quick smile, that citrine yellow hair springing to catch the light from above, and repeated, 'but tonight I might even join you in some Ovaltine.'

They prepared it, Ashley warming the milk in the micro-wave oven; they sat on high stools that he dragged out from beneath one of Han's benches, and when they had finished, rinsed the beakers, leaving them on the draining board. 'I'm going to complete that work I brought home and do some telephoning. So cut along now to bed, and I'll see you tomorrow,' said Ashley, as he flicked her cheek with a casual finger and pointed her along to her own quarters, while he himself turned studywards.

CHAPTER SEVEN

THE next day flew past, and there was no privacy to do her phoning. The office seemed crowded with customers all the time. Julia and Jenny were busy at the counter, having to leave routine work go to the wall. Not so Christina. She typed the entire day, and it was four o'clock when the last triplicated sheets were ripped from the typewriter. Julia came over.

'Finished those rotten statistics?' she enquired, and at Christina's nod, grinned hugely, saying, 'Thank goodness, even if there are other things piling up . . . but it's cover-up time now, though, so I'll help you put all these away, and they can be sent down to head office tomorrow.'

That was Wednesday, and Ashley was away when she got home. On Thursday, in contrast to the day before, the office remained calm, and Christina got on with what she had been given. Then just before lunch Julia was sent over to the mill, and Jenny was in conference with Mr Fenton.

Taking a deep breath, Christina drew the phone towards her and dialled. The familiar, breathless voice answered. Her own breath went out with a rush, and she made herself answer calmly. 'Oh, Marion—yes, it's me,' she said as the other voice came over clacketty-clack, in full spate.

'Where are you? Where have you been? Martin couldn't remember . . . he thought you'd said something about going away for the weekend. I was thinking of calling the police if I didn't hear from you soon. It's very naughty of you to worry me, you know, Elizabeth. But Martin told me not to be silly; that you knew I was away and would come home in time to welcome me back. . . .'

Yes, thought the silent girl on the other end of the phone, her stepmother would agree with that. She had been indulged and spoilt all her life and took such behaviour towards her for granted.

As the voice went on, relief came, and she got a word in edgeways. 'How's Martin?' and waited breathlessly for the reply.

'Oh, he's all right now, but. . . . Oh, of course, you wouldn't know. He was mugged, almost killed, and in his own home too!' the normally indolent voice went high.

'What . . .?'

. 'Yes, you may well exclaim "what" in that tone! As you know, I went to Sydney last Friday, and we decided, Frank, Edna and I, to go down to the southern lakes for the weekend. I rang Martin, of course, to let him know. Then. . . .' the high, excited voice stopped for a few moments to catch its breath, angry breath, too, by the sound of it. 'Then,' it continued, 'he came home on Saturday evening and thought he heard a sound—from the direction of your bedroom. He said he called out, but feeling that something was not quite right, went in. They hit him with your telephone—not a small hit, either. They could have killed him!'

'Yes,' answered her listener, 'they could have,' but her stepmother was speaking again. 'It's about time something was done about these hooligans!'

'Yes, indeed it is,' agreed her listener, who had the receiver clamped to her ear, desperately hoping no one would return to the office. 'But is he all right now?'

'Yes, now, but he's been in hospital. He's coming home this afternoon . . . but where are you, Elizabeth? Why are you away and not at the college? Martin was all fuzzy until Tuesday, that was when I got home. They couldn't get in touch with me before because, as I've already told you, we'd gone away and only Martin knew where. He told me yesterday that you'd probably tried to ring and had found no one at home. . . .'

'I'll bet he did,' muttered the girl being called Elizabeth. 'And I also bet he's worried silly about my disappearance.' Then she concentrated as her step-mother went on, 'Well, you'd better come along now, and you can help me go and bring him home from the hospital.'

In spite of the tenseness she felt, the girl couldn't prevent a small smile from forming. Yes, that was Marion! Everybody always ran to accommodate her. But not this time. She answered,

'Look, Marion, I can't come now. I've got a job.'

'You've got a what, darling? I can't hear you properly. It sounded as if you said you had a job, but that's stupid. What did you say? It couldn't have been that!'

'Yes, it could. I was offered one for just a couple of weeks. As I thought it would be good experience, I took it. But of course I'm going back to college to finish my training.' Of course she would be going back, she added to herself. What else was there for her to do? And then she found herself trying to override the interrupting voice assailing her. 'Look, Marion,' she found herself saying again, as indignant words came through forcefully, 'I've got to go—my boss is coming. I'll ring you at the weekend. Bye-bye, love.'

Neither of her bosses, Jenny or Mr Fenton, was coming, but it was as good an excuse as any. She replaced the receiver and drew a deep breath. Thank goodness she hadn't killed him! Feeling no pulse and seeing blood on the side of his head, she had been certain she had.

A glance at her watch showed her it was lunchtime. She rose and closed the entrance doors which were always shut from twelve-thirty to one-thirty. Trying to act normally while knowing she would have to sit and think things out, she made tea for them all, then took her lunch out to the garden. Sinking on to a bench set under a leafy tree and hoping the other two would decide to eat in the staff-room today, she took out a sandwich. It was left untouched, the memory of that Saturday night crowding out all other thoughts and actions.

She lived with Marion, who had married her father when she was eight years old, and Marion wasn't at all the story-book type of wicked stepmother. She was plump, smiling, lazy and charming. She had been just as charming to her stepdaughter, Elizabeth, and had made their home a happy home, putting herself out not in the slightest while doing so. The import—export business her father owned—and which she herself intended to enter when she had finished college—provided them all with a comfortable existence.

Then her father had been killed in, of all things, a stupid accident at work. Lost without a man to take care of her, Marion had just drifted into marriage with the man the trustees had appointed to manage the company. He was ambitious, and to give him his due, since he had married Marion and moved into their home, he had improved the business no end—and also, she told herself now, had been pleasant to live with.

But, growing from a young girl to an attractive teenager, Elizabeth had sometimes felt uncomfortable when catching a speculative glance unexpectedly. She had told herself she was imagining things and gone on enjoying their pleasant way of life.

Then, a week ago, Marion had gone to Sydney to see her sister who had been ill in hospital. And, wondered the girl sitting there, sandwich held uneaten in her lap, had it been her own fault that that frightening scene had happened . . . or had Martin planned it so? But, she decided definitely, he certainly hadn't meant it to get out of control as it had.

He had been lying back in one of the big lounge chairs when she had arrived home on Saturday night, drink in hand, watching television. A group of their particular crowd had been swimming and had eaten a

ake-away dinner on the beach. Then, deciding to go to
disco, they had all gone home to change.

Martin had risen, gone to the drinks cabinet, and said
asually, 'Would you like a drink, Elizabeth? It's early
o be going along to bed yet.'

But she had merely hurried past him, saying
arelessly, 'Not now, Martin, I've got no time. We're
oing to a disco. I only came in to change,' and she
eaded out of the lounge without a backward glance.
3ut he had caught up with her in the bedroom
loorway, and catching hold of an arm, had swung her
ound to him. 'Of course you've got time for a drink,'
e remarked. 'You've been out all day, you shouldn't
e going out again now.'

She had laughed at him, saying, 'Don't be silly,
Martin. Look, I really do have to hurry and get
Iressed,' and she moved into the bedroom, pulling off
he dress she was wearing over her bikini.

Whether it had been her offhand manner, or the
learness of an attractive young girl—and one,
noreover, with the minimum of clothes on to boot—
he didn't know. She didn't know, either, then or later,
f he would have carried out what his manner
hreatened. But with one arm around her, the other
umbling at her bikini top, she had been terrified, and
ad begun to fight him off. His head had come down,
ut a struggling, twisting body had caused it to miss its
nark. Breathless, frightened in earnest now, caught in
hat hard, strong grip he was exerting, she reached one
rm out behind her as they crashed into a night table,
nd seeking fingers had found the phone. With what
trength her awkward stance could summon, she had
it him from side on.

He had fallen like a tree cut down, collapsing to the
loor with a thump. A hand over her mouth, she had
gazed down in horror. What had she done? What in the
name of heaven had she done . . .? She dropped to her
knees, fumbling for a pulse, and could find none.

Unaware of what she was doing, she had returned th
dress over her head. Even if he wasn't dead, went he
scurrying thoughts, just think how this dreadful affai
would affect Marion ... think of the scandal of it! Sh
would have to get away. She didn't think of money, sh
didn't think of clothes; she only didn't want to b
caught here with this ... this. ... And anybody coul
come along at any time. After all, it was Saturday nigh
and they often entertained, or went out with friend
And—God, there were voices echoing from th
driveway now, this moment!

She grabbed up the beach purse she had bee
carrying and ran—through the side path along to th
beach. On the familiar sand she ran until she wa
breathless, then sank down with her back to
bulwark. She realised, when she had her breath bac
and could think a little more clearly, that sh
shouldn't have run, but she had been so frightened
and the enormity of what had happened ha
overwhelmed her. And now nothing would make he
go back.

In the bright sunshine of this beautiful blue an
golden day, she shivered, the ripple passing through he
entire body. The shudder brought her thoughts back t
the present.

'There's one thing,' she muttered wryly to hersel
'and that is that I can leave the penthouse. I haven't t
worry now about any scandal Ashley might make
What would he do if she simply walked away? An
what would *she* do? Without him, her life would remai
empty of love.

No one else's hands would be able to brin
forgetfulness of the world as they flowered the spac
around her with ecstasy and passion, no other lip
caress her with such slow heartbreaking desire. ... Sh
sighed. Well, that was something she would have t
learn to live with, but ... a small whisper inside he
said, 'You need not leave; you can go on as before.' Bu

of course she would have to tell him ... of course she would.

Because one day, if she didn't, inevitably she would bump into someone who would know her by her real identity. And the thought of the expression he would assume if that happened.... She shuddered for the second time in as many minutes. It would be her knowing deceit that he would view with distaste. He mightn't mind—well, he probably mightn't mind, if she told him everything herself. Memory surfaced of his kindness when he had told her he could help on the night he had taken her into the mountains for dinner.

Still, the thought of looking into his face, the thought of even having to mention such a sordid episode to him, drew the breath from her body. She couldn't. She would watch her chance and go away ... but not just yet, went her thoughts, please, not just yet....

'Christina!'

Startled, she jumped. She had not even been aware of her surroundings, so deeply had she been immersed in her miserable thoughts. Julia was waving to her from the office side-door. 'Hey, time to start work,' she called.

Waving back, Christina became aware of the untouched sandwich in her hand. Dismayed, she realised that her whole lunch remained in her case. She would have to get rid of it in the office rubbish bin. She couldn't take it home to let Han see it. Crumpling the lot back any which way, she shut the lid and returned to work.

It was only some minutes later when Jenny came through with a sheaf of papers, saying, 'Leave what you're doing, Julia, and do these. They should only take you about an hour. Mr Fenton said you're to catch the three o'clock bus, then take them in a taxi to our solicitors—they need them. Here's ten dollars for the taxi fare to there and home. Now hurry like a good girl and finish them.'

'Too right, I will, and I'll take a taxi there, but I'll splash the rest on little me, and take a bus home.' Julia flashed an impudent, happy smile at her senior, and got to work. She left within the hour, giving the girl still typing a flippant wave.

Christina finished her quota of work, sorting and stacking it. At finishing time, Jenny stuck her head out of Mr Fenton's office, calling, 'Off you go, Christina. I'll be working late. Mr Fenton and I are finally going to get rid of that backlog of stuff so disgracefully left. See you tomorrow.' She turned back into the manager's office without more ado.

Collecting her handbag, giving an all-encompassing glance around to see that everything was tidy, Christina went through the staff entrance.

Han wasn't leaning against the Holden's fender as usual. He appeared to be reading behind the wheel, apparently engrossed. Opening the passenger side door, she leant down to greet him, saying, 'Hi there. . . .' and broke off, her mouth falling open with shock. Finally she managed, 'What are you doing here?'

A smile made its appearance on the tanned face. 'Ought I to remind you, my working peasant, that I have every right to be here? I own the place.'

'So that's why you weren't. . . .' she began, and, aghast at what she had been about to say, abruptly stopped speaking.

He looked her over, saying softly in that slurred tone he could assume when he was being nasty, 'Don't imagine I wasn't standing outside the car because I care about being recognised. I go anywhere I please, do anything I want to—always. Now, are you going to get in, or stand out there all day?'

Angry at that tone, furious at what he had implied, even if it had been what she had been thinking, she stepped into the car, sitting stiffly in her own corner. 'Put on your seat-belt, Christina,' ordered that hateful voice.

More than furious with him now, she fumbled sideways and couldn't reach the wretched thing. An arm went right over her, a body leaning across her own. He had effortlessly collected the belt and she heard the snick of the catch as it snapped shut. Her breath came out raggedly.

The station-wagon was edging along the gravelled road, out through the gate and on to the bitumen. Gazing sideways, the girl seated so close wondered what was different about him—because he did look unlike his usual self. She turned and looked openly, trying to fathom out why, and said without volition, 'You look different.'

'Do I now? What makes you say that?'

And suddenly she knew. That incredible hair was as she had never seen it before. Windblown, all over the place as if it hadn't had a comb through it for a week; also, he was in jeans and a knit shirt which was far from clean. She couldn't believe it! Before, always, she had seen him only immaculate.

'Would the fact that I've been working have anything to do with it—working, I might add, since before you were up. Would it be that that makes you think I look different?'

'You might be looking different, but that rotten voice and that obnoxious tone is yours,' muttered Christina wrathfully.

'Actually,' he was continuing, ignoring her comments, and his tone had returned to normal. 'Actually,' he repeated, as he carefully manoeuvred the car around a big semi-trailer loaded with timber, 'I've been going the rounds of all my companies. The cement one, early; the glass and joinery complex, after that: the brickworks which is my largest firm: and the mill here. I've been here for the last few hours.'

'I didn't think you worked. . . .' Oh! Aghast a second time in as many minutes, her hand went up to cover her mouth. 'I mean,' she stammered, 'I thought you only went to an office and gave orders.'

'Oh, that I do! Frequently. But I also go the rounds of what I own. They're mine! And I intend to keep them that way. I'll take you out one day to see the brickworks, Christina. They're so vast, and produce so many kinds of different coloured bricks. I get an offer for them a dozen times a year, but there's no way anyone else is ever going to get hold of them—or any of my other companies.

'Accountants tell me I should lump them together in one complex and sell them as a public company; that I'd make millions. Why should I do that? I already make millions—or at any rate, whatever the government allows me to keep of those millions.

'I find ways, however, to cheat the government in some small manner—quite legitimate ways, I hasten to add. Every member of all the companies I own gets a bonus, probably itemised as overtime at Christmas. It only takes off the top some of what we make. But instead of giving it to the government in company tax, I give it to people I know.'

Glancing at him, Christina noted the matter-of-fact statement. His manner took no credit for doing such a thing. It was still another facet of the character of this man called Ashley Carlton, and she sat in her corner thinking about it, about this apparently softer side of him. Would it be in evidence when, if, she told him her story. She shied violently away from the thought of it.

'Okay—out!' his words interrupted her reverie.

Upstairs, the door closed behind them. The owner of the place stood, throwing a bunch of keys from hand to hand. He gazed at her and smiled, and the girl watching him wondered what was coming. 'Do you think, Christina,' he asked her, 'that once again you can pay for your board and lodgings by making me some tea? I haven't eaten since six o'clock and I'm starving. Han had to go to the restaurant today, and although, if I know him, he's provided dinner for us; I can't call out to him now to demand tea and sustenance.'

'Of course I will,' said Christina, but she glanced curiously at him. 'I expect you wouldn't know how to prepare yourself a meal, seeing the way you're looked after,' she added.

A shout of laughter answered her; a quite loud shout of laughter, which caused her to smile in sympathy. 'I really must disillusion you, my little toiler. I might not have done much for myself before I went to Vietnam at the age of twenty; and Han doesn't allow me to do much now. But let me tell you—I learnt. I can brew a dixie mess-can of tea over the most minute fire; strong, beautiful tea that tasted like nectar as you squatted in the jungle. I can cook up a meal to be proud of, in a galley pitching on mountains of water as our yacht runs before a howling gale. . . .'

'Do you sail, Ashley?' she interjected, thinking of the small sailboats she had crewed for herself.

'It was the love of my life . . . once, to crew on one of those ocean races was the height of my existence. It takes second place now, however. . . . About that something to eat?' he broke off their conversation abruptly.

She passed him, going to the kitchen, throwing her shoulder-bag on to a bench. Familiar with things now, she soon prepared the tea-pot, the kettle was switched on, and she gazed about her. On the table sat a long french loaf swathed in tissue paper. What could be more satisfying for just now, it being not far off dinnertime? she decided, and ripped off the fragile wrapping.

Cutting one end off in a long hunk, she sliced it down the middle, then opened the fridge. Like Han himself, everything was in its place, and on the top shelf she saw plastic-wrapped plates and dishes which were evidently their dinner, and, lower down, a plate of sliced pink ham, with beside it a small bottle of English mustard. Han had clearly known that his employer would come home 'starving' and had made suitable preparations.

Christina spread butter, added mustard, then the delicious-looking slices of ham, leaving the crusty lengths of bread open.

Suddenly, gazing at the tempting snack, she unexpectedly felt 'starving' herself, and remembered abruptly the possible reason for it. No lunch at all, but she pushed back in her mind the reason why she hadn't wanted to eat that meal. For now she would do as Ashley had asked her to—take every day as it came, one at a time. As if her thoughts had conjured him up, Ashley was coming through the archway, hair combed, and by the look of it, face freshly shaven, but he still wore the same work clothes.

As he glanced down at the second two smaller lengths which she had just finished fixing for herself, his grin showed satisfaction. 'Good,' he said. 'You're joining me. I'll carry these, you bring the tea.'

Companionably they ate their food, Ashley talking about the mill, the different timbers, Christina following some of it from knowledge gained by working in the office. Finishing her bread stick, she pushed her plate and empty cup away, and sat back. But Ashley pulled the pot across to pour a second cup for himself. He drank it in three swallows, rose and said,

'We'll dump this mess, Christina, then go and freshen up with a swim—in the ocean this time. Oh, first—Han said you were to take that dressing off your leg, and that he'd left what he called a puffer on your dressing table. You're to spray the wound with it night and morning, and leave it undressed. How is it progressing, by the way? I haven't seen it since the night I caused it to happen.'

'You didn't cause it to happen,' his companion interrupted him decisively. 'I was the one who caused it to happen. And it's getting on very well.' She made to leave the kitchen, but hard fingers on her arm stopped her.

'I think I'd like to see it, Christina. Put your leg here!' He had dropped to one knee and was patting the horizontal length of thigh that that posture brought into being.

She began to shake her head, but meeting that gaze upon her, spoke instead. 'Really, it *is* getting better. I'll take the dressing off and use this new stuff of Han's. He said, too, that swimming in sea-water would only do it good.'

'Show me it, Christina!' The tone brooked no argument. So, perforce, she bent and slipped the strap of her sandal from behind her heel and laid a bare foot on the jean-clad leg.

His citrine-fair head bent low, and she gazed down at it, not seeing his two hands come up. They caught hold of the elastoplast dressing—and ripped!

Christina yelled.

'Don't be a baby,' he told her. 'That didn't hurt.'

'It dashed well did hurt!' she retorted. 'And I tell you, Han never did that to me. He was always careful and gentle.'

'But then Han wouldn't hurt a hair on your head.' Ashley had spoken absently, unaware of what he was saying, she thought, watching him gaze searchingly at her leg. He looked up. A deep frown had come to furrow the space between his brows. 'I don't like the look of this at all,' he told her. 'I'm going to ring my doctor.'

Unsteady, balancing on one foot, conscious of those hard fingers gripping the calf of her leg, Christina couldn't break away. However, she spoke just as forcefully as he had done. 'I don't want a doctor to look at it. It's getting better all round the edges, as you can see; it's only that centre bit. . . .'

'It certainly is that centre bit. It's a nasty deep crevice filled with pus.' He put down her leg, and rising, said, 'I'm going to ring Phillips now.'

'I don't want a doctor, Ashley,' and she spoke in a

louder tone to him than she had ever done. 'I really don't want one,' she repeated more quietly.

'But it's like this, Christina,' that slur had come to take over his voice now. 'You either behave like a dignified patient co-operating with a doctor hoping to get healed, or you meet him screaming, held down as if you were my slave-girl kept here forcibly for my pleasure! Which is it to be?'

Gazing at him, hearing that tone, she realised pleading wouldn't help, and she definitely didn't want to see a doctor. She said sweetly. 'Oh well, if you haven't any faith in Han, by all means call your damned doctor.'

Ashley laughed. 'Do you think you can manipulate me in that fashion, Christina? Allow me to tell you that I have every faith in Han. But I don't like the look of that mess there.' He gestured downwards.

Given hope by this new tone, she replied quickly, 'Look, Ashley, if you'll give me until tomorrow night, I promise I'll meet your doctor with the compliancy of a very well-mannered patient . . . please!'

For a silent moment they stood gazing directly at one another, then, 'Very well, but it will have to be a good deal better than it looks now. Go and get into your bikini.' He turned away abruptly and left her.

Yes, there it was! Her glance had gone immediately to her dressing-table as she entered her bedroom. Taking up what looked like a bulb of black rubber with a thick steel needle protruding from it, she squeezed—squeezed too heavily, as the white powder spread not only where it should have covered, but all over her leg as well. More gently, she pressed a second time, allowing the—whatever it was—to conceal completely the still suppurating part of the wound.

'There,' she told the black bulb, 'go to work. You'll be washed off presently, but you'll be puffed again all over when I come back from swimming!

'I'm going mad,' she muttered to herself, 'to be

talking to an inanimate object like this!' And determinedly she marched off to don her bikini.

When she walked into the long room, Ashley was not waiting at the entrance door as she had found him on previous occasions. He was sitting slouched on the sofa with long bare legs stretched out in front of him, head thrown back against a cushion, eyes closed. She waited at the intersection of the corridor and the living room, undecided about proceding further.

Suddenly the eyelids flew open, and the blueness they covered showed intense, brilliantly stimulated, with some emotion she couldn't define. Before she had time to ponder on it further, that foreign expression had vanished, his gaze focusing. 'I really didn't expect you so soon. Usually, when waiting for the female of the species, one learns as time goes on to wait patiently,' he told her as he looked her over—no make-up, hair only combed, the same much-worn bikini covering the lightly-tanned body, feet casually pushed into the scuffs she had worn on coming here, and the big towel dragging from her hand.

Ashley was rising slowly to his feet, but she spoke across to him a little acidly. 'That's a myth, Ashley, you know. Women are just as punctual as men.'

And the man's reply came just as tartly. 'You might be pleased to think that, Christina. I, on the other hand, have reason to know otherwise.' He unlocked the door.

As they walked the few paces to the Esplanade and jumping down on to the silver sand, unexpectedly, all the complications of her life seemed to recede. This was familiar territory—the fine sand warm beneath feet from which she had kicked off footwear, buildings rising to the sky behind. And waves holding colours that were unique to this particular beach, blues that were turquoise, greens that were emerald dissolving into jade, milky-white tips taking on a translucence as rays from a setting sun caught them for that infinitesimal second. Christina glanced up, her face to the hazed lavender softness which had come to disperse the brazen azure of molten daytime—and found Ashley watching her.

The directness, the intensity of his gaze, startled her, bringing a deep flush of colour to her cheeks. But before she could drop her towel and run down to the water, a voice behind her, so close, that she jumped and automatically spun round, said, 'Hi there, Ashley. You're going in a bit late, aren't you? We're packing up in ten minutes or so.'

Standing at their shoulders were two very large, very bronzed lifesavers. It had been the younger one who had spoken, and with the brash assurance, too, that the importance of their job gave to them.

He was receiving a return grin from her companion whose hand had come out to grip her arm as he waited to answer. 'Oh, I don't know about that, Frank, my boy. It's not sunset yet, and,' Ashley threw out a hand towards the ocean in which heads were still bobbing about, 'we'll have company. Also,' he glanced from the younger to the older more mature man, 'don't you think, Peter, that I'm quite capable of performing your duties if I have to? I did them for long enough, remember!'

Ashley received a glinting white smile from a dark, tanned face, and the older man answered slowly, casually, 'I should imagine you can, Ashley. One never forgets a thing well learned—but you should remember advice we've all been given; and give. The worst time to swim is sunset and sunrise. Still . . .' his smile widened and his gaze swept over the man to whom he was speaking, then overflowed towards the young girl being held so tightly, 'go and enjoy your swim before we do leave. Ciao!' A hand waved, a smile reached out towards Ashley, and so did another smile reach out— from the younger of the life-savers. It wasn't directed at the man, however; it rested admiringly on the girl beside him. He also waved and said, 'Ciao,' but added, 'Maybe I'll see you around?'

'And maybe you won't, if I have anything to say to it, Frank. I keep my acquaintances away from any contact with your lot; memories of bygone years advising me to do so.' Ashley laughed, waved them away, and then turned towards the ocean.

They swam, and dived, and surfed, and as Christina shot one wave on to the beach, she found Ashley beside her. He stood up; that hair without colour as it lay sleeked flat with salt water. His hand went up to shade eyes that looked inland between the buildings, and finding no glinting sun-rays, he said, 'Enough, I think, but it does something for you, doesn't it?'

Still breathing a bit raggedly from being knocked over and dumped by a large wave she hadn't seen coming, Christina laughed up at him.

'Yes, doesn't it?' she agreed happily. 'But I was careless and got dumped. I thought I'd never get upright.'

'I know!'

She stared at him. 'You couldn't know! You weren't around.'

'I could know, and I was around!' His tone changed and he said, 'Come along, it'll be dark soon,' and they stepped through the clear shallows that preceded the frothing lace at the water's edge. And as they walked to where their towels were lying, Christina saw, somehow surprised, that it was full dusk and would soon be dark.

Before she could bend for her towel, her companion had done so first—not to collect his own, but hers. He dropped it round her—and despite the small knot of life-savers standing nearby who were beginning to carry on a desultory conversation with him, rubbed her wet body thoroughly back and front. For all the world, reflected the girl standing so compliantly between the hard warming hands, as if he was a trainer rubbing down a horse just in from a training gallop; utterly impersonal . . . a means to an end!

'There. We're going for a walk, and the evening

breeze gets up a little more strongly at this particular time.' His hands had left their self-imposed job and he was gathering up the two pairs of scuffs, dangling them from one hand, his own towel slung carelessly over a shoulder. They strolled, she noticed, away from their own unit, northwards. The beach was emptying, the families mostly gone, but there were still tourists and the young cramming in every precious moment of sand, sea, and warm tropical weather.

Waves sang at one side of them as they sauntered barefoot across the smooth fine sand, with lights beginning to make a fairyland of the esplanade on the other. They didn't speak, and Christina walked in silence, content.

CHAPTER EIGHT

As on the previous few days when her eyes opened on what was now so familiar territory, Christina thought for a moment, then remarked to the empty bedroom, 'It's Friday, and Ashley told me while we were eating dinner that he would have left for Brisbane before I was up and wouldn't be home until Saturday lunchtime.' Had he gone?

They had finished their meal, rinsed and stacked the dishes in the dishwasher. Ashley had gone into the living room to turn on the TV for some late news. A documentary came on immediately after, and they had stayed to watch a little white polar bear growing up. At its conclusion Chrisina had risen, telling her companion, 'No, thank you,' to another programme, needing to get away from such close proximity in the otherwise silent apartment. As she turned away to go to her room, Ashley had said casually, 'Oh, I hope, Christina, that you haven't forgotten we're dining with Uncle Edmond and Aunt Beth on Saturday night?'

'Oh ... no, Ashley!' she had protested, actually having forgotten that suggestion on the first day she had arrived here. 'Oh, no,' she had repeated. 'I don't want to go. I'll know nobody there.'

'Do you know, Christina,' a slurred voice was answering, 'I've been called a few things in the thirty odd years I've been around, but I don't think I've ever been called a nobody before.'

'Oh, Ashley!' Anger coloured the frustration of her reply. 'You know I didn't mean that. But you said the guests were business associates from Melbourne. What would I have to talk to them about?'

'Oh, didn't I tell you? Actually, there will be a girl

there, around your age too—the daughter of the chairman of the company which is interested in buying some land I own. You're two of a kind . . . well, no, I shouldn't say that! I would think you're two of a different kind. . . .' He paused, and she didn't trust that glinting expression in the blue eyes opposite. Coming to know him, and his moods, a little by now, she wondered what had caused that look of amusement.

'How can we be two of a different kind? That's a contradiction in itself,' she told him curtly.

'Well, you're both beautiful.' He broke off, laughing at her stare of amazement. 'Don't you think you're beautiful, Christina? That life-saver on the beach this evening did.'

'Don't be stupid, Ashley! *I'm* not stupid. Of course, seeing me, he might try to make a date. Of course I know I'm not unattractive. But I *am* only that – averagely attractive. I'm not beautiful, whatever this other girl might be. And if she's who you say she is, we would have nothing in common. Whatever would we discuss?

'Um . . .'

Christina stood there, beginning to get furious at the strange noises emanating from him, then he said, 'I was just trying to remember from my youthful days, what the girls then discussed. I think, I only surmise, mind you, that they talked about their boy-friends, their dates, their boy-friends. . . .' He laughed and threw up his hands at her expression. 'Okay, okay! Look, seriously, Christina, we have to go. These people had me to dinner in Melbourne and this affair is only to reciprocate hospitality.'

'But not me, Ashley. You. . . .'

That slur in his voice was suddenly very much more pronounced. He said. 'Yes, you, Christina . . . with me. And now to bed. I've had the devil of a long day, and I'm going to have a longer one tomorrow!' He walked away, moving past her door, and was nearly at his own at the end of the long hallway, when a wail echoing down it pulled him up short. He spun around, alarmed.

'I haven't anything to wear ... not to a formal dinner, which this affair seems to be.'

She saw him, and she could have hit him for it, doubling up with laughter as he opened his door. All he did was call back over a disappearing shoulder, 'Oh, I expect you'll find something. Goodnight, Christina.

She sat up in bed now with her knees drawn up to her chin, arms hugged round them. What was she going to do? she wondered. She *could* leave the mill today and go home—if only to collect clothes and money before finding somewhere else to live—and she could imagine the expression that would come to rest on Ashley's face if she did such a thing; to run away without even speaking to him. And whatever were his reasons for keeping her here, he had been nothing but kind.

She wouldn't leave. Actually, she knew she didn't want to. But after this weekend she would have to decide something. She stopped worrying about what she should do and fell to just thinking of Ashley ... the way he would sometimes look down at her and smile, the way ... She shook her head. Why did he want her here? Why not let her leave? Every day, every night, she had asked herself that. Twice he could have made love to her—completely. Her head went down more tightly against her hunched up knees. And he had walked away.

Had he done so because in the last resort he really didn't fancy her: because there might have been consequences he just wasn't prepared to take into consideration; or ...? But then why not let her go? She just didn't understand.

A knock coming on her door jerked her head up from her knees. Startled, she gazed at it. No one had knocked on it since the first morning. Hadn't Ashley gone?

Han's voice was calling quietly, 'You're late, Miss Christina. Are you up yet?'

'Oh yes, Han—sorry. I'll be five minutes.'

Bounding out of bed, she had the swiftest shower she had ever taken. Cotton-wool balls to dab carefully on her leg to dry it, then puff, puff, and the white powder was covering it completely. She thought the deep groove didn't appear so wide this morning, but told herself sharply that that idea was probably wishful thinking.

Briefs and bra, the jersey office dress swirled quickly over and down her head because it was easy to pull on. Sandals, hair combed and lipstick applied, she caught up her handbag and flew from the room. Han was standing waiting for her, a glass of orange juice in his hand. 'Drink this, Miss Christina,' he told her, holding it out. 'And here's a piece of toast to eat in the car. But first, although you really are late, I want a look at that leg.'

For the second time a man went down on his knee before her, and fingers came to clasp the back of her leg. Suddenly, out of the blue, a thought struck through her. What an unaccountable emotion was this thing called love ... attraction! One set of fingers caused the same sensation that a doctor's might; a shoe salesman helping with the trying on of shoes, whereas Ashley's ... Ashley's.... She dragged her thoughts away from him to concentrate on the words Han was speaking, satisfaction colouring his tone.

'Well, you're spared the doctor's visit tonight, Miss Christina. I was under the strictest orders to get him here if that abrasion was showing no improvement. It is ... so we'll dispense with his visit.'

'Oh, truly, Han?' Christina's voice ran high, relief as well as thankfulness sending it up. 'You don't realise how happy that makes me. Here,' she thrust the glass, empty of its contents, back at him as he returned to an upright position, and continued, 'Never mind the old toast, because I really must fly. I don't want to be late, I really don't,' and deep inside her she knew the particular reason why she didn't. She wanted no one to think she couldn't complete what she had undertaken.

'You must have been extra tired,' Han was saying as he handed over her lunch case, and she just nodded. She couldn't tell this calm, efficient male that it had been daydreaming of his employer that had made her late, not tiredness.

The pattern of the day coasted along as had the other three before it. Julia handed round chocolates brought from an exclusive sweet shop with her taxi windfall. And, surprised—because although aware that this was a job, and she was performing it as a good clerk-typist would, somehow Christina had not expected to actually receive money for it – she took the envelope Jenny handed to her as they sat down to have their lunch.

'Pay-day,' the senior girl had said matter-of-factly to them. 'Only four days in yours, I'm afraid, Christina,' and she reached over to hand Julia her envelope. Christina opened hers as Julia was doing, and exclaimed, a little embarrassed, 'Golly, I'm rich!' and stuffed it all back in its container.

At the end of the day, for more than half the drive home, Han was not very talkative, and the girl beside him was content to just sit and think her own thoughts. She realised that this episode in her life would have to end, and soon. But she had determined today to just let this weekend go by and enjoy her time with Ashley. What had he said to her once? 'We'll see what our tomorrows bring.' Well, she would see what her tomorrow brought.

'Miss Christina?'

Christina turned, surprised. She had never heard Han speak tentatively before. 'Yes, Han?' she enquired, when he didn't continue. 'What is it?'

'I was wondering. . . . You know, Mr Ashley is away. I was wondering,' he repeated, 'if instead of having dinner at the penthouse, would you care to come and have it at my restaurant? It's not that I am needed there, you understand. I am quite happy to prepare and serve your meal at home. I thought, however, as you would be alone, you might enjoy coming out and having it in different surroundings. I must warn you, though, it is no four-star place, merely a restaurant where customers can get a good meal at a reasonable price. There is also a takeaway section. Actually,' he suddenly took his glance from the road in front for a brief second and smiled at her, 'we have found it a very lucrative part of the business since we installed it. Oh, and my wife will be there!'

'That settles it, then. I'd like to meet her very much, but. . . .' her throat was suddenly constricted, 'but what about Ashley . . . your Mr Ashley? What would he say? Would we be allowed to do that?'

'Of course,' Han sounded surprised. 'He knows I intended to ask you. He only stipulated that it was to be what you wanted to do!'

'In that case . . .' laughing outright at him, Christina answered, 'I do want to,' and she settled back happily as the car drove through the busy city centre and into the underground car park.

'Give me ten minutes, Miss Christina,' said Han, as he made off kitchenwards. 'Just come as you are, but you can freshen up while I attend to some chores I need to do.'

Walking through the bedroom and on into the bathroom, Christina lifted her foot up on to a chair, and, balancing on one leg, stood gazing at it. Should she wash it with disinfectant or just puff powder over it as it was? Then, as Ashley's face swam into her vision, she reached up to the medicine chest, withdrew the Dettol, soaked some cotton-wool balls into its diluted strength, and patted. Slowly the congested powder came away, and she thought that really, this time, she was not imagining it. It *was* getting better. Drying it just as

gingerly, she used the black rubber bulb, squeezing
carefully until the powder lay thick all over the wound.
Hands washed, she paused before the dressing-table to
comb her hair, wishing for the umpteenth time that she
had a brush with which to brush it, and then she
thought suddenly, I've got some money. I can buy one
now.

What was she to do about the money she owed
Ashley, however? There wasn't enough to repay him
and have some left to buy brushes. Of course, if she
went home—no, when she went home, she could return
it. But for now, if she was going to this formal dinner
tomorrow night, she needed make-up, especially eye
make-up, and also to have her hair done at a salon—if
she could get out.

And what about a dress? She moved over to the
wardrobe and withdrew the one in which she had
arrived. It was the only suitable one there, she realised
that. That little cheeky sailor collared striped one, she
couldn't wear to a formal dinner. Critically, she gazed
at the one she was holding. It did have a beautiful cut;
it was strapless, even if it was not an evening dress.
Well, it would have to do. And suddenly she wondered
why she was worrying. It was Ashley's concern. It was
his damned dinner party. If he wanted to take someone
unsuitably dressed to an important business affair, that
was his bad luck. A flood of relief washed over her. The
whole concern was in his court.

She grinned as she caught up her handbag. At least it
had money in it now—money she had actually earned,
no less. She was still smiling as she walked out to meet
Han. He must have finished what he had called his
chores, because he was walking towards her down the
long, lovely room.

However, she averted her gaze from the slot which
was empty of its normal occupant, and wondered
abruptly where the Jaguar was at this precise moment.
Was it driving around Brisbane with another passenger

beside the driver—a beautiful passenger? Was it in a garage while its owner was closeted with business men in important offices, or standing outside a house in one of the newer suburbs, with its owner being entertained inside, or making up one of a lively pool party? She would probably never know! And she wasn't going to think about it now, either. She was going to a Vietnamese restaurant to enjoy a dinner of exotic food—if she knew Han.

She noticed that when the car got among the traffic on the main highway that they turned south. She asked, 'Where is your restaurant, Han? Not here in Surfers, then?'

The quiet laugh that was all she had ever heard from her companion—even when he and Ashley had been laughing and talking about their experiences in Vietnam that night on the balcony—came. 'Heavens no, Miss Christina. Surfers Paradise's real estate was, and still is, beyond my means. It's at Burleigh, and not on the main drag, either. Still, we have quite a good position.' He had been driving along among the thick traffic, when suddenly he braked and turned into a side street.

Christina saw it before Han could speak—a very big sign on top of what must once have been a large, old-fashioned house. Han had to take his chance among more than a few vehicles parked on either side of the street. And when she got out, with Han's fingers lightly on her arm, guiding her, she saw that there were two small cement paths leading to two large openings.

Beside him, as she entered, she was amazed at the seeming bigness of the place, and then saw that the original partitions between the house and verandah had been demolished, giving a look of spaciousness to the whole enclosure.

It was to the restaurant side that they had come in, with polished rails dividing it from the clamorous swelling noise of the crowded takeaway section. At going on for six o'clock this was already packed, with

young men and youths in their skimpy swimming briefs,
with arms around their just as scantily clad partners;
men from offices and banks, by the look of their
clothes, calling in for a quick meal to take home; elderly
women with children having their pick of the dishes
written up on a blackboard. All kinds of people were
there, and all were talking to one another over the soft,
country-style music that was playing. Sealed cartons
were issuing from a long narrow hatchway, price and
matching number stuck upon them. All this, Christina
noted in fascinated interest, and it was with reluctance
that she obeyed the insistent fingers on her arm.

The working area of the complex was just as busy.
Two men in starched white aprons, each behind his own
stove, several more at a long table, were chopping; two
women were packing and sealing the cardboard
containers as they slid towards them. Han spoke, and
all faces turned towards him, all busy hands stilled.

'This is Miss Seaton,' he told them in English. Some
nodded and just smiled. Some, the younger ones
mostly, said, 'Hello', in the same language. Then Han
had switched to his own tongue and Christina knew he
had mentioned Ashley, because his name sounded the
same in any language.

Abruptly, the kitchen had returned to busy people
working, busy hands chopping, stirring, filling, and
putting into the waiting hands of customers the
carefully prepared finished product.

Two youths at the far end were speaking quietly
together, and although it was in Vietnamese a sentence
one spoke sounded as if they were discussing films. One
word echoing across to her sounded like 'Mayerling',
which she herself had only recently seen on television,
about the Austrian Crown Prince Rudolf. She smiled
and turned to Han, and just as suddenly stopped;
abruptly the entire atmosphere of the room seemed
changed, voices stopping. Every face seemed to be
looking at the young speaker.

And then in the next second the atmosphere had seemingly returned to normal, as if for only that frightening moment they had all been caught in a camera's shutter. Han turned to guide her away, and Christina went with furrowed brow. What had just occurred concerned her, she knew without understanding, then Han was telling her, 'Come and meet my wife, Miss Christina.'

She glanced up—and saw framed in the doorway a face that almost took her breath away. It was smiling gently at her, and a soft voice said, 'How do you do, Miss Seaton?'

Finding nothing to answer for the moment, Christina just looked, until Han told her, 'This is my wife, Su-lin.'

'Oh,' her glance swung away from that lovely face before her to say, 'she's beautiful, Han,' and then she thought how remiss it was of her to be addressing him. She turned back and smiled, her most outgoing smile, saying, 'Hello, Su-lin. I'm very happy to meet you. It's like meeting a film star; and you speak English as if it were your own tongue.'

Su-lin answered, saying, 'Yes, I went to school here for some years,' but a faint touch of pink had swept upwards to creep across her exquisite magnolia skin. Magnolia skin which was broken by two eyebrow arches of ebony, and almond eyes only slightly tiptilted showed beneath a black fringe that went straight across her forehead. The lips speaking to Christine were sculptured as exquisitely as the skin was toned. All this, and the girl standing there had been endowed with the perfection of a willow-slender figure.

'Thank you, Miss Seaton. You are very kind. I really am. . . .' A slender hand went fluttering upwards, and Christina unexpectedly realised that she had embarrassed her. But Han was speaking some words in Vietnamese, and the beautiful face lit up as she looked at him. She turned and smiled at Christina, then departed with the tray she was carrying.

'Come along, I'll show you where your table is.' Han's glance had left his wife and he was moving towards the restaurant doorway. Christina said as he seated her, 'Your wife is very beautiful, Han.'

'Yes, she is,' he answered, and somehow his tone carried a sombreness that was not at all the tone of a man accepting a compliment. 'Yes, she is,' he repeated, 'but not nearly as beautiful as her sister was.'

'Oh?' Christina glanced up, beginning to say she couldn't imagine anyone being more lovely, but Han had snapped his fingers and a young waiter was placing in front of her the preliminaries of a meal she never afterwards could describe. She never knew, either, what it was she drank. The lovely Su-lin had come with a tall crystal glass frosted with ice, and when asked about its contents, she had just shrugged in her pretty way, saying, 'I don't know, Miss Seaton. Han said to bring it to you, and that you wouldn't find it too alcoholic. I must go,' she had added, and hurried away as if she didn't want to stay talking.

'Miss Seaton', Christina had noticed; not the way Han addressed her. So also had the manager called her when Han had brought him over to her table—an elderly grey-haired man with a very bad limp.

Leaving quite early, she had thanked everybody she could, and then settled contentedly in her seat as Han drove the short distance home. She wondered, grinning, what she would be eating for dinner at Ashley's aunt's place, tomorrow night, and decided that it would have to be good to compare with what she had just eaten.

CHAPTER NINE

WHAT would she do? She lay drowsing in bed, knowing that as it was Saturday morning, Han would probably not disturb her. It wasn't, however, about leaving this place that she was worrying this morning; it was about a dress and that wretched dinner. On arriving home last night, she had measured her own dress against her. It didn't cover the nasty-looking abrasion which would be so noticeable. The little cheeky dress was even shorter.

Would she ask Han to drive her to the same shopping complex where she had bought that, and buy a long dress with the money she had earned yesterday? Bother! She didn't know! She swung her legs out of bed, dragged on the despised yellow towelling slip-on over a pair of briefs, then gathered up all the clothes she had worn through the week. Whatever happened, fire or flood, or not knowing what to wear, the ordinary, mundane chores of living were always there waiting to be done. She combed her hair and wended her way to the laundry.

Han was not in evidence and the penthouse was silent. Her undies in the machine, Christine switched it on, then hand-washed the fragile blouses and the jersey dress, hanging them to drip-dry. When the short cycle ended, she transferred the garments into the dryer, then went into the kitchen. She would dearly love a cup of tea, but would never think of invading Han's domain while he was absent—not without the excuse of having to make tea for its owner.

She walked out on to the balcony, standing at the guardrail to look down. Surfers Paradise was gearing up for what it was all about—a very big weekend coming up, by the signs of the traffic. The gold and blue morning would certainly bring out the sea- and beach-lovers. Her elbow on the rail, chin cupped pensively in her hand, Christina gazed out over what was a glittering scene—windows glinting in the searching rays of the sun, cars of all makes rushing along in streams of eye-catching colours, swimmers and surfers already beginning to crowd the azure waters below.

She heard Han's voice behind her, and turned to go looking for him. He wasn't in the kitchen, however; the sentences coming from further inside. Thinking of a cup of tea, she started towards the dining-room archway. The door into the study was standing wide and she saw him speaking on the phone—the first time she had ever seen it in use, apart from its urgent shrilling which would always abruptly stop as the recorder took over.

She made to withdraw, but at his next words, stayed there silent, unashamedly eavesdropping. He was speaking to Ashley's uncle, and anything she could learn about tonight she would!

'I'm sorry, Mr Blythe, that's all I can tell you.' There came a silence in which the listening girl could hear an angry voice coming from the receiver quite loudly. She grinned as Han lifted it away from his ear, then spoke himself.

'All I can tell you is that when Mr Ashley rang from Brisbane yesterday, I gave him the message which you had left on the recorder.'

More distinctly now, the tinny voice echoing across the miles of wire could be distinguished. Then Han's again.

'I don't know where he is now, Mr Blythe,' and Christina grinned again as she noticed the word 'now'. Of course Han mightn't know at this precise moment of time where his employer was, but. . . .

'Don't give me that for a tale, Han!' Ashley's Uncle Edmond was interrupting. 'You know everything that goes on around that damned place. All I want to know is, who is he bringing? Is it that stray he's picked up?

And ...' the voice on the phone went even higher if that was possible, 'is she still living there? His aunt doesn't want her whole dinner spoilt, and that boy of hers shouldn't worry her.'

'That boy', thought the girl, thinking of Ashley. Heavens!

'Mr Blythe, I'm sure Mr Ashley wouldn't want to worry Mrs Blythe. He really has told her he is coming—and with a partner. He just told me to ring and confirm it after I found your message on the recorder.'

'But who in the hell is he bringing—that's what I want to know!'

'I am not aware of all Mr Ashley's plans, you must understand, Mr Blythe. I. . . .'

'Is that waif of a girl still there ... living there, I mean?'

And how are you going to get out of that direct question? wondered 'that waif of a girl'.

'There is no one around here at the moment, Mr Blythe. But you do realise that I am at the restaurant and at my own home with my family a great deal of the time. And as Mr Ashley went to Brisbane. . . . Look, I must go. He will see you tonight and you will be able to take up with him anything you might want to know. Goodbye, sir.' The receiver was gently laid down, and Christina wondered if the irascible voice at the other end of it had finished all he had to say.

She was still grinning when Han walked out and saw her. He shrugged. 'You know of course that I would do anything for Mr Ashley. But Mr Blythe is a nice gentleman. I don't like having to put him off.'

'And of course he knew you were doing just that. I've never heard such a diplomatic way of lying through one's teeth!' Then Christina's voice sobered and the smile went from her face. 'Will they hate me going, Han? You know I really don't want to go.'

But if her smile was gone, there was one back on the face opposite. 'Shame on you, Miss Christina! Do you imagine Mr Ashley would walk in among his own people and important business executives, if he wasn't satisfied that everything would be as it should? Now, I don't know about you, but I've been busy this morning, and I deserve a cup of tea after that session of just a moment ago.'

'I came in to ask you if I could make myself a cup. I don't want anything to eat. 'However, she should have known. Orange juice was handed out of the fridge, embedded in its little bowl of crushed ice. Toast was made, tea carried to the small table in the kitchen nook—and not marmalade, but a jar of preserved cumquats. Christina had used cumquat jam before—hadn't everyone in Queensland?—but she hadn't tasted this elixir from the gods, these whole preserved cumquats that squashed into jelly when spread on toast.

Glancing at her watch, she saw that it was going on for eleven o'clock. They ate in companionable silence, and she drank the second cup of tea Han poured for her, then said, and this time it was her voice that was tentative:

'Han . . .?'

'Yes, Miss Christina?'

'Do you think . . . would it be possible for me to go to a salon to have my hair done? At least then that will be something that will be in keeping with the occasion.' The last sentence was said a little bitterly.

With no answer forthcoming, she glanced swiftly across at him. But there wasn't refusal stamped on his face; it was more as if he was considering something. Then he said, 'What sort of salon had you in mind, Miss Christina? Just one to wash and set your hair, or an exclusive salon to style it as well as shampooing?'

Astonished, she grinned, saying, 'My, you are up to the fashion scene, Han! But what the hell, we'll live dangerously. We'll plump for the exclusive one, shall we—that is, if I can get into one of those establishments at such short notice.

'Oh, I'm sure that won't be any bother. I'll use Mrs Blythe's name. She is a very valued client at the one I have in mind. . . .'

He was interrupted. 'You simply can't do that, Han. Goodness, what if they were to check?'

'Pooh, who is going to check? The only thing they will be interested in is if you can pay their bill. The thing is, can you pay, Miss Christina? I can. . . .'

'No, you can't! I got my first pay-packet yesterday, and although it's not in Ashley Carlton's bracket, it will certainly pay for a shampoo and style-set in even the most exclusive salon. How do I get in touch with them?'

Her companion, however, had already risen to leave, and she heard him in the study telephoning.

Returning in an incredibly short time, he told her, 'They can't fit you in until around two-thirty, Miss Christina. They have two weddings today which will keep them busy as well as their normal bookings. Will that be suitable?' Han's voice carried a touch of anxiety.

'That will do beautifully. I can wallow in a bath before I go. Because if I know them, they'll be late and it will be towards five when they finally spray the last curl. I couldn't have received a better time if I'd had my pick of them. I'll go collect my clothes from the laundry now, and see if there's anything else that I can set about to make myself beautiful.'

Suddenly, that last word being spoken caused her to think of it, and she said, 'I've really never seen anyone as beautiful as your wife, Han. I'm sure that sister you mentioned couldn't have been.'

His hands stacking the dishes, Han was turning away, but he said as he passed her, 'Yes, she was, Miss Christina. She had just that extra something that caused all eyes to follow, all men want to know her . . . to wonder about that air of fragile beauty.'

'You seem to be speaking in the past tense. Does that mean she's not here in Australia, or that she. . . .'

'She is not here in Australia. She died in Vietnam.'

Han departed, and somehow his tone stopped any more questions she might have liked to ask.

There wasn't much she found she could do in preparing to make herself beautiful, decided Christina. She had no cosmetics, having needed all Ashley's money for necessities. Delving more earnestly inside the medicine cabinet, she still only came up with shampoo, hair-conditioner, powder and bathsalts, and she pounced upon it—a nail file, its pristine newness enclosed in a hard plastic shield. At least, she thought, she would be able to file her nails, even if she had no varnish with which to paint them.

So, taking it, and the historical romance she had chosen what seemed a long time ago, she sat in the chair by the window. She did file her nails, but the book remained unopened in her lap. Ashley should soon be home; he had said about lunchtime. She lay back, dreaming, and as once before when there had come a knock upon the door, she jumped, startled, then thinking it might be Ashley, she ran to open it. The excited look of welcome faded as she saw that it was Han, not the man she had been hoping for. Nevertheless, she smiled, asking, 'You wanted me, Han?'

'Actually, no, I don't, Miss Christina,' he was smiling at the acute look of disappointment she was trying to wash from her face. 'I've just brought this package for you. Mr Ashley was here for a few seconds only to deliver it, but he had to leave immediately. He said for you to be dressed by six-thirty as he wants to arrive early to introduce you to his aunt before the other guests arrive.'

He almost had to thrust the big, deep, cardboard carton into arms which made no effort to take it, then he turned to leave, calling over his shoulder, 'Don't forget I have to take you out around two. I'll bring you a snack meal here on a tray for lunch, as I am going to be busy.' Christina was calling out to him not to bother about food—but he had turned the corner of the corridor.

With her large parcel clasped loosely, she moved inside, kicking shut the door with her foot. For quite some moments she didn't open it as it lay staring back at her from the foot of the bed.

Then untying the ribbon with which it was fastened and pushing aside the tissue paper covering whatever lay within, she drew out a dress.

'Oh!' The breathless word echoed around the empty room, unexpected tears stinging behind her eyelids. It was the most fabulous, the most beautiful thing . . . a creation! She raced to the wardrobe to find a hanger so that she could admire it more completely.

It was high-necked at the back, and, from what she could distinguish, cut very low in front, the long full skirt falling from just under the bustline and having a six-inch frill around the hem. Tiny puffed sleeves tied with apricot ribbon bows completed a dress that had been cut by a master . . . and oh, it was lovely! Created in a floating white chiffon layered over a pale apricot underdress of pure silk, it shimmered and gleamed with every movement—and could have emerged directly out of a Regency ballroom. Christina could imagine one of the high-born ladies of that era moving down a grand staircase to go dancing in it.

But could *she* go dancing—or rather, dining—in it? Yes, she could. Nothing would prevent her wearing it.' The arrogance of that Ashley!' she muttered suddenly. He *could* have told her! Worrying all that time about what she should wear. . . . Then words Han had spoken echoed. Of course he wouldn't have arrived at a dinner held for sophisticated guests accompanied by someone he would have to feel less than proud of.

She touched a fold of the delicate overdress again, and watched the shining ripple as it passed through the dress. She wondered where it had been bought. It was obviously made to order, by the looks of it. And the size was exactly hers. As he had once intimated, Ashley certainly did know his way around feminine apparel. But what in the name of heaven had it cost? She shook her head. She'd think about all these things after the weekend. She swung away from the dress hanging there and danced over to the window to pick up the book which had fallen when she had jumped to open the door, hoping to see Ashley.

She stood there right across the room, her considering glance still upon the creation hanging upon the wardrobe door, knowing that the way she wore her hair wouldn't suit at all. Her shining blonde mane would somehow have to be put up. Then a big smile split her face, so that it looked young and mischievous. Thanks to Han, she had an appointment. A place like that could do anything with hair. She would just demand a Regency style.

She danced across the room again to open the door, an excited happiness making of her a different girl from the one she had sometimes been while living here. Han smiled when he saw her, then handed her a tray, saying, 'You had no need to worry, now did you? You should have known!'

'And you should have told me. But of course you wouldn't have, would you? That would have been Mr Ashley's business.' Nevertheless, she took the tray held out to her, and before she could close her door Han had disappeared. Certainly a man in a hurry!

Christina ate some of the cold meat and salad without even tasting it, but suddenly she smiled. Fancy a dress having such an effect on one's whole metabolism! Still, she defended herself, it wasn't only having a beautiful dress to wear; it was the fact that she would be able to go with whom she was going, and know she would look—well, not exactly beautiful, but more than a little attractive.

Carrying the unfinished lunch back to the kitchen, she smiled at the place around her, thinking she could be walking through a sleeping palace dreamed up from a fairytale. No sound disturbed the quietness, not even the faintest murmur of traffic or outside noises penetrated. She looked and saw that the big glass doors were shut.

Back in her room, she danced past the dress and on into the bathroom. Both taps on and half a bottle of bath-oil tipped into the running water, she screwed her hair on to the top of her head and stepped down into the tub. Languorously she lay, allowing the water to run until the foaming froth reached up to her chin, then leaned over and turned off the taps.

Taking up the large natural sponge, she smoothed it over her skin, feeling the oil-laden fragrance relax her entire body. She lifted a slim tanned leg from out of the mass of bubbles and gazed at the wound marring it. It looked worse, but that was only because it was soft from the water, she told herself. It now covered a much smaller surface, but that groove would still need more time to mend and would probably always leave a mark. She lay gazing at it, knowing, as she travelled down the long tunnel that carried the years of time, this was one scar that would forever bring memories . . . one brand of Ashley Carlton's that she would always carry.

She sat up, a nymph rising from an ocean of foam and pulled out the plug. She wasn't going to look any farther than tonight. Out and wrapped in a large towel, she padded into the bedroom. Slipping on her watch, she saw that it was after two, so donning the freshly-washed jersey dress, she let down and combed her hair, then making sure the money was still there, she left the room.

Han was not in evidence, so it was her turn to sit and wait. She wasn't kept long, however. He came hurrying along almost immediately.

Stopping the car in the middle of Surfers to allow her to alight, he told her, 'Look, Miss Christina, I have business to attend to. I'll come for you around five o'clock. If you are finished before then, you'll wait until I come, won't you?'

She heard the anxiety that coloured his tone, and smiled at him. 'You haven't anything to worry about this afternoon,' she told him. 'Nothing is going to prevent me from wearing that dress! Don't worry, Han.' She flipped a hand in farewell, and he had slid off into the traffic.

Inside the luxuriously appointed reception area, Christina had to stand back as what was probably one of the wedding parties erupted into it. Three attendants and the bride, she imagined, by the look of them, although not yet in their wedding clothes. They left and she made her way to the desk. Receiving only an enquiringly raised eyebrow, she also said only, 'Miss Seaton.'

'Oh, yes, Miss Seaton. We've given you Mrs Grey, our head stylist, but she'll be occupied for a few minutes yet. Will you take a seat?' Christina was ushered into a comfortable modern chair, handed magazines, smiled at, then left to herself. She smiled. Hadn't she told Han this would happen? She wasn't left long, however. A girl came along, asking, 'Miss Seaton?' and at Christina's nod, said, 'Come with me, please.'

She did as she was bid and settled into a cubicle, where she was joined by an elderly lady who, with an all-encompassing look at Christina's casual hairstyle, said, 'Well, my dear, how would you like me to set it?'

With a deep breath, Christina took the plunge, saying, 'I'm wearing a Regency-style dress. It's very simple, but very beautiful. Could you style my hair to match it, please?'

The woman smiled at the glowing but slightly anxious face. 'I think we might be able to manage that,' she said gently. 'Go with Gloria and she'll shampoo it for you. Use a highlighter on it, Gloria—you know the one,' she told her young colleague.

'Yes, Mrs Grey,' the girl answered, and bustled Christina away.

Back in her cubicle with a towel wrapped head, Christina sat and waited. And when Mrs Grey did arrive, she was all business. 'Now,' she began, 'let's see what we can manage. Yes ... yes, I think curls beginning from the top to cascade down the back of the head; one side swept tight to furnish that needed hair, and ... mmm ... for the other side—yes, just two curls ... two ringlets, I think, one to fall down on your neck, the other to lie against your cheek. ...'

'Oh!' interrupted Christina. 'Ringlets? Won't I look silly?' Alarm coloured the words. Goodness! She would hate, worse than not having a suitable dress to wear, being made to look stupidly out of fashion, or, more undesirable, trying to look like some silly, simpering teenager.

'My dear,' Mrs Grey's voice had risen too, 'you're going to Mrs Blythe's home to a party. You're having your hair done at this salon. Do you imagine we would allow you to go from here and not be a credit to us? Now. ...'

After that severe voice speaking those words, Christina subsided, listening unhappily to the murmurs issuing from the two women working about her, one asking, the other obeying. She gazed once at the mirror, and noticing the strange way the rollers were going in, looked abruptly away. She then thought defiantly that she could always brush it out and trust to luck that it would curl under as it usually did.

'There! Put Miss Seaton under the dryer, Gloria,' and suddenly glancing at Christina's face, Mrs Grey said, 'Miss Seaton, you'll look lovely, I promise you. From how you described your dress, you were in love with it. You'll be in love with your hair the way I've styled it just as much. Is it to be a big party tonight? We know Mrs Blythe quite well. And ...' here her smile suddenly went wide, 'we've had her nephew calling here at times.

Do you know him?'

Oh yes, she did know him, thought Christina, and then she remembered Han, and said, 'She has several nephews, Mrs Grey. Which one are you referring to?' and hoped to heaven that there were other nephews.

'Oh, I mean Ashley Carlton, of course. I wonder which one of his harem he'll be taking there tonight? Well, we haven't done her hair this time.'

Oh, haven't you? thought Christina, as the woman turned to listen to the receptionist who had come to murmur to her. Then, with one last word to her assistant about keeping a close eye on Miss Seaton's hair, she left the cubicle.

Christina lay back under the dryer, wondering where Ashley was and what had been the business that had kept him about it on a Saturday afternoon. And when had he actually ordered that creation hanging back there in her room, because one thing she was sure of, he hadn't just walked into a department store yesterday and plucked it off a line.

Then Mrs Grey was bustling back, and Gloria was taking out rollers and pins. Almost frightened to look, when she did, all Christina could see was a mass of curls hanging everywhere. Mrs Grey turned her chair around, probably so she wouldn't see the fright she was going to look, thought Christina dismally, as she sat for what seemed years, being combed and pinned, hearing the muted talk above her head. Finally that assured voice said, 'You can look now, Miss Seaton.'

Almost cringingly, Christina turned and looked. Her glance flew up to meet the smug, satisfied gaze which Mrs Grey was bending upon her.

'Satisfied?'

She was unable to reply. She looked beautiful! Even if the style gave her the appearance of stepping out of another era of history. Her fringe was swept back, and starting from just above her forehead were a cascade of curls falling down to her nape. There was no hair—as that witch had said earlier that there wouldn't be—on the right side of her head, that being used in the cascade. On her left were two shining ringlets, one to lie against her neck, the other to caress her cheek. And that apprentice *had* used a highlighter. Her hair would never have the charisma that the colour of Ashley's presented, but. . . .

'Yes, thank you,' she told the smug face reflected in the mirror behind her. 'Oh, yes, I am, but will it look too much for just a dinner—even an important dinner?'

'From how you described your dress, I wouldn't say so. Anyway, to look charming—on any occasion—is more than permissible. You'll have to be careful what make-up you use, though.'

'Oh,' said Christina again, thinking of what she didn't have. 'Do you . . . do you sell cosmetics as well as hair preparations here?'

'We do. However, we only keep the one brand, and it's. . . .'

'That doesn't matter,' answered Christina, guessing at what the pause conveyed. Hadn't she only previously made a remark about living dangerously? 'Could I see them, please?' she added.

And, at a few minutes to five o'clock, she went into the reception area, a small parcel clasped tightly, an even smaller amount of money in her purse, but her face wearing a happy, satisfied smile.

She saw Han leaning indolently against the front of the salon, and as her presence must have darkened the doorway, he looked up, his glance passing over her to go beyond, and then abruptly swinging back. He looked at her and his smile widened. 'How charming, Miss Christina,' he told her. 'Have you got any money left?'

She returned that knowledgeable smile, answering, 'Not much, but do you think it was worth it?'

'Well, I am not up in all ladies' hairdressing fashions; my wife always has hers done as you saw it. Are you asking me if I wonder how Mr Ashley will like it?'

As she nodded, he laughed, saying, 'No doubt in the course of the night he will tell you himself.' Han gave a quick glance at his watch.

Inside the penthouse, he remarked casually, 'Mr Ashley must be home.'

Puzzled, Christina glanced round. Everything seemed as usual. But if Han said Ashley was home, he was! So she took to her heels and fled. She didn't want him to see her before she was entirely dressed.

Slipping off the wrappings from her pile of jars and tubes, she gazed happily down at them. Protesting that she was wearing apricot when Mrs Grey had suggested green eye-shadow, she had been overridden. 'It will bring out the green in those amber eyes, Miss Seaton,' the head stylist had said. So, as she had been right about the hair, Christina had bought it. But for now, she picked up the apricot shade of nail varnish and went to sit over by the window to paint her toe and fingernails. Passing the bed as she did so, she stroked the evening bag—no, the reticule, she told herself—which had been included with the dress—because certainly a modern-day handbag wouldn't have suited it at all.

Bent over double, tongue caught between her teeth, she painted first one set of toenails and then the other, holding both feet out to scrutinise her finished handiwork, then she dealt with her fingernails in the same manner.

She knew she had better make a start to get ready, but found her hands were shaking. She hadn't seen Ashley since they had had dinner together after their swim and walk upon the beach. What if he had met one of his former ... friends in Brisbane? What if he had changed his mind about wanting to take her tonight and couldn't find a way of getting out of it? What if . . .?

Determinedly, she rose from her chair and padded across the room to begin dressing, and it was just before her given deadline that she stood gazing at herself in the mirror, at a face which carried a shine from the foundation; at cheeks blushed with just the faintest touch of pink; at eyes shaded out a little further to her temples, the colour appearing to make the green-flecked amber show a deeper green. She had used the brush from the square case of lipstick with a heavier hand than normally, outlining her lips carefully. And her hair. . . . The painted lips smiled, causing one shining ringlet to dance against her cheek.

CHAPTER TEN

THE man lounging casually on the carved arm of the sofa turned his head. For a full moment he stood, then the lids came down, hiding any expression. Almost immediately they flew upwards again, and far back, the girl standing there looking anxiously across at him saw a gleam in the blue eyes, startling in its intensity. She asked:

'Does it look all right, Ashley? Do you like it?'

'And how am I to answer that? Do I imagine I'm dressed in knee-breeches and bow deeply from the waist, or do I do this?' He walked the three steps and taking hold of her hand, raised it to his lips. 'I'm overwhelmed, Christina. You look charming . . . out of this world—isn't that the cliché?' That gleam was still there, but he was smiling now, his teeth flashing white against the bronzed skin as he said, 'I picked right, didn't I, with the dress?'

'Indeed you did, except for one flaw.' Her hand went up as it had done in the bedroom to try to tug the décolleté higher. And she snapped angrily as he laughed, 'It *is* cut too low. I don't like it!'

'I should imagine other people might, however; the male sex, for instance, me included.' He smiled at her outraged expression, saying only, 'I told them I wanted something different, young and charming, but not too demure. Apparently they thought that that one—what did you call it?—flaw, would counter-act the simplicity of the whole dress. I didn't specify what I meant by it being not too demure.'

'You might not have,' she returned, a stain of red which was not the blusher colouring her cheeks. Uneasily, she watched his glance roam over her, over the swell of her breasts rising white and firm from the built-in bustline, then she said, almost stammering, 'Before, I thought it the kind of dress a young girl might wear going to her first ball. Now I feel like Lady Caroline Lamb, who was happy to flaunt herself, and her . . . charms before any assembly!'

This time Ashley was laughing outright. 'I assure you, my dear Christina,' he was telling her, still laughing, 'that after one glance at you, no one would mistake you for Lady Caroline Lamb! Now, shall we go?' He had moved to unlock the door, and looking at him, suddenly Christina felt a surge of love well up within her, reaching out towards his unconscious figure. She might, as he had said, look charming, but he . . . oh . . . devastating was the only word to describe him. Black trousers and bow tie, with a white dinner-jacket that seemed to show up his skin a darker shade. And crowning it all was that fair citrine-streaked hair which gleamed with its own charisma as the light caught and played upon it.

He had turned, and an eyebrow rose, as he saw her still remaining by the sofa. 'Coming?' he asked, and she walked slowly across to him, the apricot silk underdress whispering as she moved, the white chiffon floating about her.

It was still daylight as they drove down the crowded Saturday evening highway; but the sun was thinking of going to bed as it took with it a band of vivid scarlet and crimson towards the horizon. Even as she watched from out of her side-window, Christina saw it slide over the edge of the world . . . and the swift twilight gather.

She said, 'The colours are beautiful, aren't they, Ashley?'

Her companion laughed. 'I don't know about that,' he remarked prosaically. 'On the ocean, sailing, we often think those violent colours presage not the best of weather. But how have you been occupying yourself in my day and a half's absence?'

'Oh, didn't you know I'm one of the world's toilers? Unlike some people, I couldn't just cut and run to the big smoke and enjoy myself. I had to work on Friday. Today, I washed, loafed, and I got my hair done. . . .'

'Yes, you did indeed do that,' she was interrupted.

'Should I have had it done in a more conventional way, do you think?' she was beginning in a slightly apprehensive tone, and was interrupted for a second time.

'No, I don't think so,' he said, and without taking his glance from the road, continued, 'I wouldn't dare begin to tell you what just looking at you does to me at this particular moment, because we have a business as well as a family dinner to get through, so. . . .' Here, for the briefest second, he swung his glance to her, and she saw that indescribable gleam was still there, far back in the blue of his eyes, darkening them.

Then he had braked and swung off the highway to enter a sidestreet. They travelled on it for only a few minutes, then stopped before a pair of large scrolled iron gates, which swung open silently to allow them passage. Round a circular driveway they went, to pull up before a long, doubled-storied white house.

Ashley helped her to alight, and as they turned towards the porticoed-columned façade, he said, 'Well, here we go to face the Lion's den. Are you ready, Christina?' She turned to look up at him and saw in the reflected light his laughing face and brilliant eyes, and it was her hand that went out involuntarily, and his fingers that came to clasp them. Meeting his mood which, from the time she had walked out to meet him, had appeared to hold an exhilaration she couldn't define, she laughed back at him and said, 'In this outfit, I can outface any Lion's den!'

The large studded door had opened before they reached it, and an elderly man in a dark blue suit said quietly, 'Good evening, Mr Carlton,' and nodded to Christina as he made to guide them towards an open

door from which a blaze of light was spilling. But a
figure had come quickly from it, and Ashley's Uncle
Edmond was saying, 'Oh, there you are, Ashley'—but
he had spared not even a glance for his nephew, swiftly
turning to look at the girl Ashley was holding. His eyes
widened, and his mouth almost dropped open.

A voice holding more of that peculiar slur in it than
Christina had ever heard, said softly, 'Your mouth is
open, Uncle Edmond! You remember Christina, don't
you?'

'Yes, certainly. . . .' And taking the hand Christina
was holding out, he answered her gentle, 'Good
evening, Mr Blythe,' with a stammered, 'Yes, my dear,
and how are you?' Apparently not wanting a reply, he
quickly began to usher them into a long drawing room.
Not one but two women came forward to greet them.
The elderly, smaller one looked at Christina with
Ashley's blue eyes, albeit faded a little, and for a
moment didn't speak, then with one all-encompassing
glance at her nephew she took both Christina's hands,
and drawing her forward and kissed her cheek, saying,
'So this is Christina—welcome, my dear.'

Mystified at such a reception, Christina only
murmured a conventional greeting. She hadn't expected
this, and she turned for elucidation to her escort. He
was receiving a kiss too. The younger woman had
reached up to salute his cheek, saying, 'Hello, Ashley. I
bet you didn't expect me to be here?'

'No, I didn't, but I should have known,' was his
somewhat enigmatic response.

'Yes, you should have. Mother felt she needed
reinforcements—for this important business dinner, you
understand,' and giving a gurgle of laughter, she turned
towards Christina.

'My cousin Elva, Christina.'

'Hello, Christina. I love your dress. Am I allowed
to tell you that, or am I too outspoken for a first
meeting?'

Christina didn't know what to answer, but then she saw the cheerful smile and the kindness behind the words. She smiled back, but before she could reply there came the bustle of an arrival, and Mr Blythe caught Ashley's arm, drawing him out into the hall.

Four people were entering with their host and his nephew in what seemed a crowd. And then behind them appeared a fifth, towering head and shoulders above them. Mr Blythe was bringing the first two guests across to his wife—the man self-possessed, easy, with the assurance that power and experience gives, the woman beautifully groomed, as assured in her own way as her husband. And arriving next between two men, one of them Ashley, was the girl who he had told her was somewhere around her own age. Her hand lay possessively on Ashley's white dinner-jacketed arm; her face turned up to smile and be smiled at.

She's older than I am, thought Christine, looking across at the doorway where the couple were outlined, and quickly sent up a prayer of thanks that she was wearing what she was, and, looking as she did. For this other girl also carried the poise and assurance that both her father and mother had . . . and she was attractive— attractive in a way Christina would never be—in the way she acted, in the invitation she was so obviously extending to the man whose arm her hand rested on. As dark as Christina was fair, with a cloud of hair hanging below her shoulders, caught back from her forehead with two diamond stars. She was wearing a dress of azure jersey which clung to every curve she had—and she had curves!

'I thought we might endeavour to make Alicia's stay more interesting for her while she's up here,' said Ashley, after he had introduced the two girls,' by producing others of her age group, so. . . .' but here the dark girl interrupted, smiling dazzlingly up into his face as she said for them all to hear.

'There was no need for that, Ashley. I would have

been more than happy to have only you to escort me around.'

'Flattery will get you nowhere, Alicia,' there was laughter echoing in Ashley's voice. 'And you won't say that when you see what I've brought you. Ted!' he called to the fifth person who had entered and who was being welcomed by Ashley's aunt and introduced to the southern visitors.

'Ted Vestrie, Alicia.' He lifesaves as well as crews for ocean yacht races, and he's just been transferred to Melbourne. I thought it might be nice for him to meet you before he goes down there.'

Alicia was polite, and charming to him in an offhand manner. Who wouldn't be to a husky, bronzed, six-foot two lifesaver? But it was Ashley in whom she was interested, Ashley whose figure she followed as he moved off to help his uncle with drinks. Alicia had a small crystal glass handed to her, the sherry glinting amber. Christina was also handed a crystal glass by fingers she recognised from seeing them across the table at meals for the last few days. It was not a small sherry glass, however; it was a tall, long-stemmed one. And although it also held an amber liquid, it had shining, effervescent bubbles rising glintingly upwards. Before she could look up to say thank you, a head of pale gold bent, and a voice said softly in her ear, 'Just a touch of brandy—enjoy it, my love.'

Anyone in that beautifully appointed drawing room looking on would merely have seen an attentive host handing a drink to one of his guests, and that guest not glancing up, only nodding her thanks, as she gazed down upon her reinforced ginger ale.

Had he merely been using party talk? she wondered. No, she decided. With Ashley, he only said always what he meant. But 'my love'! Her fingers trembled and she quickly raised the glass to her lips. 'Hell, Ashley,' she muttered sotto voce, 'there's more than a touch of brandy in this!' But as she continued drinking it she found it delicious. Bringing her head up, she saw that their youngest visitor from Melbourne was holding court, both Ashley and Ted giving to her their entire attention, laughing appreciatively at the joke she appeared to be telling them.

Then coming to stand beside Christina was the other man belonging to the firm of Saxons. He had just lowered his glass after drinking from it. He said, smiling pleasantly at her, 'Good Scotch, this.'

He was nice, she thought, merely using the drink as an opening gambit. She answered. 'I like mine, too, even if it isn't Scotch. Is this your first visit to the Gold Coast, Mr Grayson?'

'No, I'm up here a lot on business—and the name is Rex. Actually, though, if we get this land belonging to your friend over there,' a throwaway gesture indicated Ashley, 'and build this tower block of ours, I have every intention of acquiring one of the units for myself. My wife would love to live up here. And it would be nice to have acquaintances that we already know,' he raised his glass to her.

'You realise you're talking to a Queenslander, Rex? Of course you'd want to come up here—doesn't everyone?' she laughed at him, happy at finding she could take part in the social give and take that this sort of gathering generated. It was only with one man that she found herself unable to act naturally.

There came a sudden bustle of late arrivals, the murmur of apologies. A manager of one of Ashley's companies, by the sound of it, thought Christina. And almost immediately Mrs Blythe was saying. 'Jim tells me dinner is ready. Shall we go in?'

The man called Jim might, and probably was, working for the Blythes, but he seemed also a friend by the way he was addressed, and as they moved into the large hall, he was waiting at a door opening from it, ushering them to places. Twelve of them sat down to dine, and Christina found herself placed between Rex and Mr Allison who had just arrived. Opposite them was Alicia, with Ashley on one side and Ted on the other.

'You know, if you'll allow an old married man a little leeway, I'd like to tell you how charming you look, Christina ... it is Christina, isn't it? You look as if you'd stepped out of a painting from another century.'

Startled, Christina turned to look directly at her dinner partner. But Rex's expression showed only sincere admiration. And suddenly she dimpled at him and said. 'Just as well we're sitting down, or I'd have to drop you a curtsey! Actually, Rex, I ... I had the dress, so I had my hair done to match it.' She stopped speaking and moved a little sideways to allow the white-uniformed waiter to serve the entrée.

This turned out to be succulent white crabmeat, served naturally with only hot melted butter over it. And as the meal wore on she found that this night to which she had looked forward with such apprehension was not the ordeal she had been anticipating. So at ease was she feeling that when Rex asked casually, 'What do you do, Christina? Are you still at school or university, or,' his glance ran over the exquisite dress, the elegant hair-do, 'do you just do nothing but enjoy yourself?'

'Actually, I'm at business college. I take book-keeping and typing.'

'Really? Not shorthand? That, with typing, is the most usual subject. You must have something particular in mind to select book-keeping.'

Yes, she had had something in mind. Now ... now she didn't know what she was going to do, even if she was going to stay here on the Gold Coast. She glanced up to reply—and caught Ashley's eye. His head was lowered attentively to Alicia; he was giving her a laughing answer, but his eyes were looking at Christina. And he would probably have heard her answer to Rex—and——! She hadn't told him as much. She felt the colour stain her cheeks ... and he had called her 'my love'!

Suddenly her appetite had completely fled, and setting the embossed silver cutlery on her plate, she thanked goodness the course was almost finished. She found also, though, she had the same distaste for dessert when it was placed before her. Normally, she had the healthy appetite of a teenager, especially for concoctions like the one just being set down. But she pushed her fork into cake saturated with wine, impregnated with nuts and candied fruit, covered completely with mounds of whipped cream, and left it lying there, knowing her constricted throat wouldn't swallow it. She was thankful when Mrs Blythe smiled round the table, saying, 'Coffee in the drawing room, I think,' and there was a general movement as they began to leave the table.

Her arm was taken, quite impersonally, and with Elva, she was guided over to Alicia and Ted. 'I think we,' Ashley laughed, and an eyebrow rose, 'junior members here had better stick together. I'll get involved in all sorts of business if those over there catch me. What liqueur would you prefer, Alicia?'

Jim was wheeling a coffee-laden trolley, handing out cups already prepared for those whose tastes he knew, gazing interrogatively over a poised silver pot at the guests he didn't. Christina had hers with cream and sugar—no Galliano tonight, she thought wryly, and with Alicia and Elva, had a tiny crystal liqueur glass placed beside her cup. Most of the men were holding big balloon containers, she noticed, as did Ashley too. Ted had waved a dismissing hand and was drinking only coffee.

The talk became general, but in only a few minutes it was Alicia who glanced at Ashley, saying, 'I'd like to dance. Could we go on somewhere?'

'Why go somewhere? There's a ballroom—of a sort—here. You had your coming-out dance in it, didn't you, Elva?'

'Yes, and so did Charice. Those were the days! I can't

see my daughter having a coming-out ball. However, I expect there'll be other things to take their place. I'll go and ask Mother about dancing. You do realise, however, Alicia, that we'll only have recorded music?'

'Oh, I don't care about that, Ashley will find something good for us to dance to, won't you?' Alicia's hand went on to his dinner-jacketed arm, her face turned towards him holding all sorts of promises.

A kind of shout came from the business group at the other end of the big room, laughing disclaimers from the women. Then Elva was back, saying to Ashley, 'You're to go and get it ready, but I was told to tell you that we're not having everything our own way, and that you're to put on a waltz or an old-fashioned foxtrot first. Dad wants to show off, and Mr and Mrs Saxon think they'll enjoy one dance anyway. Come along, we'll all go.'

She led them through the large hall, down a short corridor and, pushing open double doors, began switching on lights. They came blazing from chandeliers hanging from the ceiling. It was quite a big room; not a ballroom in the accepted sense, but certainly having enough space to accommodate a large party. A few chairs stood round the walls and down at one end was a group of small tables with chairs tipped up against them. And in a corner at the opposite side was a triangular dais on which stood a piano and a recording tape deck. Heavy curtains covered long windows, and the floor, Christina noticed, gleamed with a shining polish.

Entering in a close-knit group, as they got further from the door they gave the appearance of being a very small party indeed. Ashley had moved straight towards the tiny stage, Alicia having tagged along after him. He fiddled around up there for a mere second or two, then music swelled out all about them. Hidden speakers, Christina surmised. Smiling, she also realised that Ashley had done as he had been told. It was an old-fashioned dance tune that was filling the room.

Mr Blythe gave a courtly bow to Mrs Saxon, and off they went, and the girl watching had to admit that Ashley's Uncle Edmond was an accomplished dancer. Then, abruptly, her attention had left them entirely. Ashley was dancing with Alicia. 'Well,' she muttered to herself, 'what else could he have done without being rude?' Alicia had been more than at his side; she had been almost on top of him, thought Christina maliciously.

Ted was asking, 'May I have the pleasure, Christina?' and, startled for the second time tonight, she gazed searchingly up at him, then laughed as she went into his arms. 'You know, Edward,' she told him, her laughter still gurgling out, 'I've never before had those words spoken to me. I've read them, of course, but they belong to a forgotten world nowadays. How on earth did you come by them? And,' she continued, as she followed his skilful steps, 'how did you come to be so expert at this kind of dancing?'

'Oh, school, I expect,' he replied carelessly, as he swung her round. 'We were obliged to go to dances, and for our own sakes we had to know how not to make fools of ourselves. However,' here he glanced down at her from his great height, 'it comes naturally to use such words to a girl who looks as you do.'

'Why, thank you, sir,' she laughed back at him, and, the music finishing, she was swung round to come to a standstill, her lovely dress floating about her.

When Ashley returned from the hi-fi set after re-setting it, a different kind of tune boomed out around them. Mr Allison had lured Mrs Saxon into a corner and was initiating her into the rigours of disco dancing. Ted had manoeuvred Alicia into the middle of the floor, and there was no need for either of them to be initiated into performing in that fashion. They were giving an exhibition all of their own. Ashley had

approached his aunt, and even to that rhythm they were
managing to move smoothly. Besides Mrs Allison and
Alicia's father, Christina stood watching and admiring
the two dynamic figures—Edward behaving like a
dervish, Alicia following every movement and improvis-
ing quite a few of her own. However, she was allowed
to do so for only a moment. Rex said, 'I'm really not up
in all this stuff, Christina, but I'm willing to try. How
about coming over in that corner and we'll try out our
own steps?' They spent an exhilarating ten minutes and
she could thoroughly enjoy it—wasn't Ashley dancing
with his aunt and not with Alicia?

She saw Rex look at his watch after sending a swift
glance towards his boss, then he was saying, 'We'll go
along, Christina. I think Mr Saxon has had enough.'

Ashley must also have been keeping an attentive eye
on his guests. He was asking, 'Ready to go, sir? Allow
me just one more. I haven't danced with Christina yet,
then I'll pull your daughter away.' He took hold of
Christina's arm to walk her to the dais, saying, 'I'll
hang on to you while I change the record; if I don't
you'll be gone, and I, most likely, will be snaffled.'

She went into Ashley's arms as the music started; and
it wasn't disco rhythm that echoed all round the big
room. Suddenly the evening was how life should be.
This was where she belonged, cradled in the grasp that
held her so confidently. Unconsciously, she moved even
closer, moulding herself against his contours. He
pivoted, sending their bodies apart, and, leaning his
fair-golden head down to hers, he said urgently, 'Stop
it, Christina! As much as I'd like to dance the way I
want to, I can't here, with everyone in the room looking
on.' She didn't answer. She danced the rest of the time
with her hand on his shoulder, feeling his arm tightly
around her waist, and made herself content.

She stood beside the Jaguar with Ted, as Ashley and
his uncle saw their guests off, having made her own
farewells to Elva and his aunt. There was no moon and

the night around enclosed them in black velvet. Her
glance swung suddenly upwards. Yes, there it was—the
Southern Cross, blazing its own message to them down
here, its brilliant five stars standing out from the other
pinpoints of diamonds. Ted spoke, but she didn't hear
him. To all purposes, she was still in Ashley's arms,
dancing. Then he was beside them, speaking to Ted,
opening the door for her.

The drive home passed. Ashley said, 'So long, mate. I'll
see you around two tomorrow,' when he dropped Ted off.
Christina received a, 'Goodnight, Christina,' and they
were driving through the neon-brilliance of Surfers and
then home. Only silence reigned in the car. She cast a
surreptitious sideways glance towards her companion
and saw that his face wore a frown; deep furrows
indenting his brows. As they were going up in the lift, he
said, 'I'll be with Saxons all tomorrow morning,
Christina, but I promised Alicia to take her sightseeing
after lunch, then to have a swim and drinks. You may as
well catch up on your beauty sleep in the morning, then
Han will find us a scratch meal. After I deliver Alicia to
her family, I have to drive Ted up to Brisbane, and also
conclude some unfinished business at the same time, so
I'll stay there the night.' He stopped speaking while he
unlocked the door and they went inside, then he
continued, 'But I'd like to talk to you on Monday
evening. We have a few things that need discussing.'

'Ashley. . . .' her hand went out to him. 'Ashley, we
can talk now. I . . . I. . . .'

'No, not now, Christina. There are some actions that
need finalising. On Monday! Now, I'm going to bed.
Come along.'

Perforce, she went along, and stopped before her
door. He reached round to open it and switch on the
light, as he had also done on the evening he had taken
her to dinner in the mountains. However, the follow-up
of that night wasn't to be repeated. He half raised a
hand in salute and was walking off down the passage.

Unhappily, Christina walked inside and closed the
door. She went to stand before the dressing table mirror
and stare at the girl reflected back at her. Without being
conceited she knew that she looked quite lovely.
Enough so for any man to want to kiss her—even if it
was only a goodnight kiss. Sighing, she kicked off her
sandals and reached behind her to unzip the dress. It
went down about three inches—and stuck. She brought
it up again, carefully, then just as carefully slid it
downwards. It stuck again. 'Blow the thing,' she
muttered. It was a good, an expensive dress; the zip
shouldn't stick. She manoeuvred it back and forth, but
it wouldn't slide past whatever was obstructing it.
Angrily, she jerked. It stuck fast, and now wouldn't
even move upwards. Furious, she brought her arms
down to rest them, then raised them upwards over her
shoulders to begin again. She couldn't move it. Tears
now in her eyes from anger, she stood wondering what
to do. She could rip it downwards to see if she could
free it, and maybe tear the exquisite dress beyond
repair, or she could sit up in it all night and wait until
tomorrow. But even tomorrow she would have to ask
Ashley to try to free it . . . what else could she do? She
could tear it, she supposed.

She stood there, undecided, biting her lip, then
turned to walk resolutely to the door. Down the
corridor she stopped before a door through which she
had never entered. She waited, gathering her breath,
then knocked. No answer forthcoming, she knocked
again.

'Han. . .?' The voice went high in surprise.

'No. It's me, Christina!'

The door flew open and the scowl on Ashley's face
was thunderous. 'What are you doing here, Christina?'
the words were slow with the deep slur which came
when he was angry. He was tying the sash of a maroon
robe in angry jerks around his middle.

'I'm sorry . . . I'm sorry. . . .' she was stammering. 'I

really didn't want to come, but I had to! My zip is stuck
. . . and it's not just an excuse. I couldn't. . . .' Tears
were in her eyes now, actually spilling over, and the
man's expression changed, if only a trifle.

'Stop babbling,' he said, and reached out a hand to
draw her into the room. 'Now, what is it?'

'My zip—it's stuck. I really can't get it down. If you
could just ease it open for me, I'll go. . . .'

Looking directly into her face, Ashley saw her
distress. He smiled, saying, 'Let me look,' and turned
her round under one of the hanging chandeliers. His
fingers delicately tried to ease the zip both up and
down, with no more success than she had had herself.
'You'd think, wouldn't you,' she remarked between
clenched teeth, 'that the blessed thing had come from a
flea-market instead of from the expensive salon it
obviously did!'

'Which it did!' came laconically from above her. She
could feel the fingers probing and pulling. He said, 'The
zip seems to fasten both the underdress and the top
chiffon. From what I can see you've caught the bottom
half crookedly when you zipped it up. I'll have to get
my hand beneath somehow to undo that silk from the
zip teeth.' Calmly, he lifted the skirt and it was easy for
his hand to slide up under the full gathered material,
but when he arrived at the tight-fitting bustline, he
found it quite a different matter.

Suddenly Christina felt the body leaning against her,
the arm along her bare back, shake. The tremors went
right through him—and angry, furious, she knew he
was laughing. It was certainly only silently, but it *was*
laughter. She went to turn on him, hands clenched, but
his fingers came to hold her straight. He said, 'I was
only thinking, Christina, that here you are, taking the
place of the young village maiden having to enter the
lair of the lord of the manor in what should be high
drama. And just look what it's turned into! Sheer
bloody farce! Look, keep still, will you? I'll undo this

unnameable zip somehow, and without damage to your dress, either. You might need to wear it again. Here,' his tone changed, 'hold those two ends together if you can get your hands high enough.'

She took the two ends he placed between her fingers, holding them tight, and felt the hand beneath the dress wriggling more firmly upwards. The fingers twisted and turned, and suddenly there came a muted shout of 'Eureka!' and she felt the fastening move. His hand outside the dress pulled, and the zip went down smoothly.

'There,' said the voice above her, and there was satisfaction in the word. But making a grab for the side she wasn't holding as it began to slip, she found she was too late, the apricot silk slithering down her body as if she were shedding a second skin. Gazing down at it, lying in a small heap of intertwined colours, she stooped to pick it up.

'Leave it, Christina!' As she stood half bent, arrested by his words, Ashley repeated, 'Leave it. Step out of it. I want to see the reason for it not working.'

Taking note of the tone, in bare feet, she carefully stepped back, leaving the heap of gossamer on the thick oyster-shaded carpet. She made no attempt at trying to cover her sparsely-clad figure. He had seen her in less covering than this, she thought disdainfully, her bikini being more minuscule than these pants and bra, even if the briefs were white and clinging and the top a strapless strip of white satin.

They gazed directly across at one another, then Ashley walked a few steps, throwing open a wardrobe door. He threw again, this time in her direction, and she caught the white towelling robe, the one he had worn when he had taken her swimming in the pool below.

'Thank you for freeing my zip,' she told him curtly, not adding his name, and turned to go. A voice abruptly halted her. 'Christina.' She stopped, but remained with her back turned to him. 'We have some unfinished business to attend to,' he said. 'Come here.'

Slowly she turned. He was holding out a hand. Without volition she went forward to take it. He drew her down the long room, past a king-sized bed turned down for the night. No sign of silk sheets or satin comforters showed here. White linen gleamed with a pristine shine accompanying plain white pillowslips. The room was large and although it had two blazing chandeliers providing the illumination, there was an austerity about it too. Definitely a man's room. At its far end a circular cushioned seat ran inside what was probably vast picture windows, but they were covered now with deep midnight-blue curtains to contrast with the pale oyster-shaded carpet. Ashley sat down, pulling her to sit beside him.

'Now show me your leg, Christina,' and as she stared at him, astonished by the question, he said, that slur more noticeable, 'You do remember, surely, that I was to check it last night about the desirability of letting Phillips see it. Han told me it's healing. Now, let me see for myself.' Reluctant to raise her leg to the light, to his gaze, Christina remained immobile. He leant down, bringing it up to rest across a knee from which the maroon robe had slipped, leaving it bare. Glancing at him, however, she knew his only concern at the present moment was in checking the wounded leg. His brow carrying a frown, he said, 'It doesn't seem to me to be getting better as quickly as it should.'

'Yes, it is. That groove in the centre isn't so deep as it was, you can see it isn't, and the grazed skin around it is almost all better. There's only that one little piece.'

'It's not a little piece, and if I'm not mistaken it will leave a scar. I expect that's where the Jaguar's bumper-bar caught you. God, I could have killed you!'

'You couldn't have killed me, Ashley. And the whole accident was entirely my own fault—you know that!

Also, if your reflexes hadn't been as good as they were. . . .' she allowed the words to trail away.

He was stroking the side of her sore leg with the tips of his fingers, running them absently up and down the smooth tanned skin beside it. She wished he wouldn't. The contact brought to her metabolism the need to be held in his arms; the desire for his kisses. She withdrew her leg, setting it down in its original position, then made to stand.

His fingers went about her wrist, tightly. He said, his words again slow with that slur, 'Christina. . . .' He lifted the hand he held and placed his lips against the pulsing blue vein of the soft inside. From somewhere far back in a mind not really conscious of it, she was thinking what a difference an intonation could make to the way a name was spoken. But she wasn't consciously thinking; her body was only feeling. . . . His lips lifted and across only inches, blue eyes looked into amber green; looked not merely into the outward façade but deep into another dimension. Christina gasped at what she saw—the intensity, the pressure of emotion. Her own lids fell over eyes which had sent him the message that whatever he wanted . . . whatever the night held . . . was her wish too.

She felt herself lifted back against the cushions, her legs brought up on to the seat, and felt behind her still closed eyes the body that came to lie alongside her. His fingertips rested, light as thistledown, against the shut lids, on her temple . . . then began their nerve-shattering passage from jawline to throat . . . and further, to halt against the line of white satin. They remained there, unmoving, and she waited, taut, knowing the need to mould her body against the one pressing upon her, to fit herself into the curves and angles as she had done on two other occasions.

But something—a memory perhaps of him walking away from her twice before; even, maybe, a deeper instinct that had stayed dormant from some primitive

time—kept her passive. She still remained aware with
her entire being of the immobile figure lying completely
against her. Then ... then ... the fingertips lifted and
his lips took their place; her body jumped.

This time no primitive instinct prevented her. She
arched towards him, and felt her body slide exactly into
the contours of the one waiting there. His lips trailed up
from the white mounds above their satin sheaf and then
stopped at the corner of her mouth. She turned to meet
them, and as his kisses began to send their message of
need, passion, desire, into every particle of her being,
the arm beneath her tightened, while the arm above
held her to him, breast to breast, flat exposed midriff
against the naked skin her own robe had left uncovered,
smooth brown legs intertwined with strongly muscled
heaviness.

She was not only being kissed now; his hands, his
body, were using their own kind of persuasion to kindle
the leaping fire consuming them ... and now,
peremptory demand was starting to take the place of
gentleness, conscious thought disintegrating as they lay,
lost together in those slow heartbreaking caresses. And
somewhere far back was the knowledge that this time
... this time ... loving her as he was doing, he wouldn't
send her from him.

Then, incredibly, his lips had moved from hers, his
body still crushing her into the cushions, going
impersonal. And the hand which had given such delight
lay flaccid on her bare waist as if cold reason had come
to take over his emotions.

She felt the lips against her throat as his head was
turned sideways; she felt the arm heavy across her, the
one beneath her back which was even now still clasping
her tightly to him ... she felt ... but she knew he had
gone from her, and heard the muttered difficult words,
'More than anything I want to make love to you ...
but not tonight. Just bear with me, Christina.'

She answered in a voice dazed with passion, 'What is

it, Ashley? Was it me? What did I do?' And then, appalled, she thought, He doesn't know who I am . . . what I might be. I wouldn't tell him, and to him, I could be anyone . . . anything. He wanted her, that she knew unequivocally. But. . . . She swung herself off the cushioned seat too, as the heavy body rolled from her to stand upright, his head resting on a folded arm against the deep blue curtains. She said, 'I'm just an ordinary girl, Ashley; there's nothing in my past that would turn you from me.'

He made an indifferent dismissive gesture, saying curtly, 'I know who you are,' then turned and walked to a cabinet against the wall. It was not from a bottle that he poured, however. She heard the clink of ice and saw clear liquid gushing from a frosted silver jug. He downed the glass of water in one long swallow, stood for a moment longer, then swung round, tying the unfastened sash of the maroon robe.

Gazing anxiously at his face as he returned to her, Christina saw him smile, even if ironically. He reached out and brought the ends of her white gown together, then tied the belt in two swift movements. He said, 'Sit down, Christina. I knew . . . I knew I mustn't start any of these heavy love scenes. My only excuse is that I couldn't help myself . . . and you were here where you shouldn't have been. But now I'm sober and in my right senses—well, almost,' he added, and his teeth gleamed white against the brown skin as again that ironical smile made its appearance, 'and I want you to listen to me! I want to make love to you, Christina. Never think I don't, whatever impressions you may have received to the contrary. But . . .' here he halted, as if wondering what words to use, then continued, 'I've told you before that we would talk on Monday evening. There are a couple of things waiting to be finalised, but I should have them cleared up by Monday. I had . . . I have . . . call it a superstition, about something that happened a long time ago, which also, in some circumstances, could happen today. It's a nuisance, but it's there ... and there's nothing I can do about it. Now, how about going along to your own room?'

'I don't want to go to my own room! I don't care about any old unfinished business, and if I say I don't care, it's my responsibility.'

'No!' The slur had suddenly gone, the tone going so harsh that it brought her up short. 'It's *my* responsibility. And I'm thinking of my life ... my very way of living, if you want to put it that way, for all my future. Come along!'

She came because she couldn't dismiss that voice, that tone of absolute harshness. But she walked silently beside him down the long, bright, lovely room, watching him collect her dress on their way. Silently too, she went along the corridor to her own open door. Ashley stood beside it gazing down at her and his smile was wry. He reached for one of her arms, extending it himself as she made no effort to do so, draping the dress across it. Her other hand he also raised, opened the palm, pressed a kiss into it and closed it into a fist. 'There,' he said, 'until Monday evening. Trust me.' He was gone.

CHAPTER ELEVEN

THE shafts of light were entering the bedroom low down. It was very early and the sun had just risen. You wouldn't think that dust motes would dare to exist in this palace in the sky, reflected Christina. Especially when you thought of the two immaculate men who inhabited it.... Her thoughts shied away from that branch of thinking. Dark stains of violet which shouldn't have been there underlined her eyes. She had only fallen into a doze in the early morning hours and then awakened again after a short time. She had lain watching the pale dawn creep up over the land and then the bright shafts of the sun's rays make their appearance. Another blue and golden day for the coast, she thought wryly. She had a busy day ahead of her, but her plans were laid.

Remembering the carefree manner which had surrounded her on arriving home yesterday evening, she shrugged fatalistically. For the first time in her young life she knew what shock could do to one. She hadn't enjoyed the day greatly, but it had been an agreeable one. She had risen, and gazing at the lovely hair-style, remembering they were to go swimming, had shampooed it out. Then she had lunch with a charming impersonal host, who spoke to her pleasantly, looked after her comfort—and showed in not the slightest way that he remembered one second of that heavy, passionate scene of the night before.

They had driven to pick up Ted and then Alicia. They had toured the hinterland, and then the coastal beauty spots, returning for drinks beside a pool at the Chevron Hotel. But it was Ted who was her companion, Ashley being monopolised by Alicia.

Christina admitted, however, more than a little acidly, that he did nothing to discourage her. Finishing the afternoon tea brought to them under the sun-umbrella outside, Ashley had pushed back his chair, and with that charming smile, that hair which seemed to strike more like lemon gold than ever after a day in the sun, said, 'I'll take Christina home. Do you think you can amuse Alicia for half an hour, Ted? I'll be back then to deliver her to her parents while you pack.'

Christina hadn't missed the triumphant smile curving those full lips opposite, because their owner was to be taken home last and she would have him to herself for as long as she could keep him.

Well, she had been driven home, taken up in the lift, and along to her room. The backs of long, tanned fingers had stroked her cheek for the barest moment and he had said, 'I'll see you tomorrow after you come home from the mill. Take care till then.' That was all. A hand had half-waved and he had turned and left. Christina watched his figure until it turned the corner, then went inside and closed the door.

She thought of Alicia, and of Ashley going to her, then determinedly went to shampoo the chlorine from her hair, wishing yet once again that she had her blow-dryer. Which thought abruptly brought to mind the fact that one way or another, she could go home and get it. After tomorrow, she would be with Ashley ... or without him. Either way, things being out in the open, she could go home—even if only to see Marion and collect her clothes and some money.

Standing at the window, combing her hair dry, she decided to fill in the time writing to Sally. Han wouldn't be calling her for dinner just yet, and she owed her friend a reply. She and Sally had grown up together, gone to school, and told their secrets to one another all through it, until the other girl had left Queensland on her parents' transfer. Christina went out to find Han, who was busy dusting some Chinese vases kept in a locked glass display cabinet, asking, 'I'd like to write a letter, Han. Have you any materials for it?'

'You will find everything on Mr Ashley's desk, Miss Christina—paper, stamps, and envelopes. If there is none on top there will be some in the drawers.' Han gave her a smile, but went on with what he was doing.

In the study, she picked up two sheets of the heavy cream paper—and remembered with a smile the note written to her on such a sheet which she still carried in her bag—a stamp from the tooled leather case—and couldn't find an envelope. Trying the two doors on the left, she found them filled only with letters and household accounts, likewise the top right-hand one. Yes, there they were, stacked neatly on top of reams of writing paper, in the bottom drawer. She reached in for a packet to withdraw one from a bundle, and saw beneath them a framed photo lying face down.

Why she picked it up to look at it, she never knew, then or afterwards. It was not a thing she would normally have done. Perhaps somewhere at the back of her mind was the thought that it might have been of a younger Ashley. Nevertheless, look at it she did . . . and staring out at her was the face of Su-Lin . . . the beautiful face of Su-Lin. Not looking as Christina remembered her when being welcomed at the restaurant; that had been a serious Su-Lin, not this radiant young girl looking out at her now.

The countenance from which she couldn't take her eyes carried a glow . . . a glow that only being deeply, devastatingly in love could bring forth. You could not mistake it—that look on this younger Su-Lin's face. And across the bottom, written diagonally in a childish, unformed hand, were the words that kept her there rigid, unable to move.

'For my darling Ashley,
Always and Forever,
   Your Su-Lin.'

The inscription must have been written before the photo had been put into the heavy silver frame, thought the girl gazing at it, because only the end of the U in the first part of the name showed before the hyphen and the N of the last part was half cut off. Christina couldn't make herself put it down. It was clamped so tightly in fingers which showed white, inflexible. 'For my darling Ashley'. She saw the words again. There was no ambiguity about them, and 'Always and Forever', was inherent in the warmth of those eyes, the secret smile on those exquisite sculptured lips; the radiance that was shining out at her from that embossed and chased silver frame.

Emerging as if from a dream ... no, a nightmare, Christina went to replace it, and then, unable to help herself, brought it back to gaze unbelievingly again. Su-Lin's face still looked out at her; there was no way there could be a mistake. The photo went back this time, upside down as it had been discovered. Finding an envelope the last thing in her mind, she shut the drawer, and, as if a sleep-walker, turned and moved stiffly towards her own quarters. She knew Han called out to her; she knew somehow she waved to him the sheets of paper she had still had clenched unknowingly in her hand.

Inside her bedroom, back leaning against the closed door, she gazed unseeingly before her. 'What ... how...?' she muttered. Was this the reason Ashley couldn't bring himself to make complete love to her? Was he in love himself with the beautiful Su-Lin? Han's wife—*that* was the incredible thing about it. Han's wife! Han might work for Ashley, but there was respect and, yes, deep affection on both sides as well.

When had it happened, this doomed love? It must have at least begun two or three years ago. That radiant face was younger than the countenance that the girl of only a couple of nights ago had shown. Why hadn't he married her? Knowing by now something of Ashley's character, Christina realised nothing would prevent him taking the girl he loved. Hadn't he loved her enough? Had the emotion been only on her side? but.... but then, why hadn't he consummated *their* love? thought Christina. She knew she would rather be married to Ashley; that she had never thought of living with a man without being married—but Ashley was Ashley, and she would never be interested in any other man. And he wanted her, of course he did. What man wouldn't, the way she had thrown herself at him? But he couldn't be in love with her. In the final analysis, she hadn't been able to dispel Su-Lin from his mind. So he had probably decided that Christina was too young for him to involve her in a casual, fleeting affair.

Yet it all came back to 'Why?' If he was in love with Su-Lin, why hadn't he married her? And if he hadn't, and Han had, why keep that photo not even decently put away?

What would Han think on seeing that 'Always and Forever'? There was no getting away from such absolute words. Had Su-Lin married Han on discovering there was no future with Ashley? But then why . . . why had he not made love to her, Christina? The thoughts went round and round in her head. Then, abruptly, she was thinking of herself in connection with the whole affair. What was she going to do?

Even if he was about to complete that unfinished business, and it was with Su-Lin, and he came to her—what was she going to do? Words jumped out at her: 'My darling Ashley'. God! Her smile was bitter. The description about this man was hers as well as Su-Lin's.

There was no alternative. She would have to go. If she hadn't been made conversant with this so unbelievable situation, she would have quite happily fallen in with whatever Ashley suggested. But not now! She knew she couldn't. She would never lose herself in Ashley's arms after this. Su-Lin's face would always come between. What was that old cliché though about half a loaf being better than none at all? Yes, she was tempted, but that 'Always and Forever' written across that so beautiful face showed her the folly of such thinking—but it still didn't prevent Ashley's face swimming before her vision; his arms holding her feeling so real; his kisses. . . . She twisted now, abruptly, and swung her feet out of bed. Such thoughts only brought misery. She moved to the dressing-table to pick up her brush. Absently, she pulled it through hair tangled from tossing and turning all night, as she gazed down at the note she had written for Ashley.

Wondering what would be the best thing to convince him that she really wanted to put these last few days behind her, she had remembered a remark he had made once about his being around for a longer time than she, Christina, could remember, so. . . . She picked up the folded sheet of heavy cream paper with only his first name written across it, and wondered what he would say, or do, after his receipt of it. Probably nothing, she thought bitterly. She might have saved him an unpleasant explanation. It began:

'Dear Ashley,
    Having discovered there's nothing to prevent me from returning home, I'm doing so today. Thinking very seriously about us and the future, I've decided I took this time with you in too romantic a fashion— like something that could happen in a fairy story. I now believe my life will be better served living among my own friends, and my own generation.
    May I leave with you, dear Ashley, my truly appreciative thanks for all your kindness and forbearance towards me in the time I was here with you, and will you give my thanks and best wishes to Han for his kindness, too.
    I realise that at times I've been less than reserved in your presence, Ashley, but I'm convinced that the course I'm taking now is the best one.

With my thanks again for all your consideration to me, and the sincerest wish that you find all you might want in conducting your own life,
                              Christina.'

She hadn't realised that tears were running down her face and dripping over. Hastily she moved the note out of harm's way, leaning it back against the dressing-table mirror where it stood out and would not be overlooked. A hand went up to knuckle tears away and she began her preparations. Her own dress came out from the wardrobe, her bikini from where it had been washed and hung to dry after yesterday's outing. Underclothes and sandals which Ashley's money had bought, packed neatly in one drawer. It was not that she wanted to leave them behind for any illnatured reason; it was that wearing them would bring back too many memories every time she put them on . . . and such memories were those she would have to learn to live without.

Showered, and using Han's puffer for the last time, she noticed that the cause of her being here *was* almost better. Tomorrow she would go to her own doctor just for a last check. Her bikini went on; her own dress over it. Make-up used, she dropped the whole consignment of jars and bottles into the waste basket. There was no way she would ever use apricot varnish again. With a deep sigh she turned to the wardrobe, her hand tenderly smoothing down the chiffon and silk of the creation Ashley had provided for her. 'Goodbye,' she told it, and shook her head angrily as she felt the sting of tears come again behind her eyelids. She trailed her hand across the dresses she had bought with Han, then closed the wardrobe.

'I'm coming!' she called as Han knocked on her door—and went on smiling. She followed the retreating figure, thanked him softly as she was handed her glass of orange juice. She made herself eat what was placed before her because she hadn't come out for dinner last night, telling him through a closed door that she had already eaten too much through the day. Now, ploughing through the meal, pushing it into a system that didn't want it, which would have liked to reject it completely, she didn't notice the covert, anxious glances he kept sending her way. He didn't speak, however.

Declining a second cup of tea, she pushed back her chair from the table and said over a shoulder, 'I'll get my bag, Han,' and in her room she picked it up and gave a last unhappy glance around. Unhappy now, but she had been happy living in it. Hoping Han wouldn't notice her scuffs, she went out to meet him. She sat in her seat, and as she always did, glanced out at the countryside flying past, thinking, I'll miss this.

Out of her side door, she leant down to address her driver, and again felt the tears threaten as he handed to her the lunch container she had forgotten, saying, 'You don't look too well, Miss Christina. You are not ill, are you?'

Dredging up a smile, and unable to do anything else, she took the box held out to her. She said, 'You've been very good to me, Han. Thank you!' and left before he could answer.

Greeting her with almost the same words Han had just spoken, Jenny said, 'Good morning, Christina. You don't look very well. Are you all right?'

'I've had a toothache,' the unblushing lie came promptly. 'If it doesn't improve, I'll have to go to the dentist.'

'Okay, but look . . . just in case, do these first.' Jenny hurried to get a sheaf of folders and plonked them down beside Christina's typewriter.

Hypocritically, Christina gave her a painful smile, but she began typing immediately and worked energetically until, with a glance at her watch, she called out, 'Would you mind making morning tea, Julia? I'll try to get these finished and then catch the eleven o'clock bus into town. I'll have to go and see about my tooth.' She wasn't telling lies, she thought defensively. One day she would be going to get a dental check-up.

Coming over, Julia laid a sympathetic hand on her shoulder, saying, 'No, of course I wouldn't. Is it aching very much?'

'I'd like to get it seen to,' replied Christina noncommitally, beginning to feel like Delilah. In the event, she got away quite easily, and collecting her handbag and Han's lunch container, she left. She couldn't make herself leave it behind.

She caught the bus and then a taxi, hoping after checking her money that she would have enough. She did, but only just. Leaning back in the cab, she gazed out at the familiar scenes as they cruised south, and wondered if the aching loss that was all she felt now would ever leave her. Had she done the right thing? Just this minute, she didn't think so, but in the long run, in the years to come, if he loved someone else. . . . And she would always have something to remember; his charm, the charisma which had seemed to enfold and colour her life while she was with him. . . . Also, she had been granted a concept of love that she would never regret.

She walked up the steps of the old colonial house that was her home and rang the bell. Preparing to ring again, wondering if Marion was at her bridge club, as she well could be, she halted the downward push of her finger on hearing footsteps coming towards the door.

'Oh, my love!' said the plump, smiling woman, confronting her, and Christina found herself enveloped in two welcoming arms, smelling the perfume she had known for so many years. 'Come on in,' her stepmother was urging as she released her and closed the verandah door.

Following the older woman through familiar rooms, Christina smiled when they came to the kitchen, and noticing that expression, Marion smiled too. 'Yes, well . . .' she answered the look, 'I have to play bridge all afternoon, so I need my sustenance. However, I expect it will stretch to two helpings, don't you think, Elizabeth?'

After being called Christina—which was her second name—for the last week or so, it sounded strange to be called Elizabeth again. And of course the Seaton was her mother's maiden name.

'Now, my dear, what have you been up to? And what's this job you were telling me about on the phone? Aren't you finishing business college?' The questions were coming fast as Marion brought another setting of crockery to the table.

They gave Christina the time needed to put her words into order. She answered, 'The job was only a temporary one, Marion, and I'm going back to college tomorrow to finish my diploma course. But, Marion. . . .' she stopped, and reached out a hand to lay it across the plump, ringed one on the table before her, 'I'm still going to stay with my flatmates—for a while anyway. You won't mind, will you? I'll be home much more frequently now I'm at college and not working.'

'But why, Elizabeth? You're happy here, aren't you, and. . . .'

'Yes, of course. But I'm grown up now, you know,' and before the other woman could interject with what Christina saw coming, she added, knowing it would please her stepmother, 'Also, Marion, I'm going to have a talk with Martin, so tell him, will you? We'll have to see about giving him a say in how the firm is run now I'm of age. We'll work out something.'

'Oh, Elizabeth, he'll be so pleased! You're a good girl. . . .'

'No, I'm not!' interrupted her stepdaughter. 'It's you who've always been so good to me. Look,' Christina changed the subject, 'I expect you want to be leaving, and I want to pack. I'll take my clothes and leave my other things until we see what eventuates. Okay?'

'Of course it's okay, Elizabeth. As long as you're happy where you are and they're nice girls. But then you wouldn't have shared with anyone but nice, respectable companions.' Christina wouldn't call Ashley 'nice' or, for that matter, Han. But. . . . Suddenly the ache was almost too much to bear and she turned abruptly away.

She waved goodbye to Marion; she packed her clothes, ruthlessly discarding into a large plastic garbage bag garments she decided she really didn't want or need. Then she found a cardboard carton in the junk room and packed records and books to be collected when she had found a permanent address. Then, in the familiar jeans and T-shirt, she carried the two bulging suitcases to the front door, collected a very large shoulder bag, also bulging, which included in its depths her cheque book and wallet. Then, phoning the mill first to advise Jenny that it might be as well to look for another typist as she didn't know when she would be back, she rang for a taxi. She wasn't going to stay with friends at any flat, as she had led her stepmother to believe, but was going to a motel she knew of just around the corner, intending to remain there until she could decide what she wanted to do.

But first she had to go to the bank . . . and, much more importantly, she had to stop thinking about Ashley all the time.

CHAPTER TWELVE

IT was in a knot of female students that Christina emerged from college the next afternoon. Missing a week's lectures, she had worked hard all day striving to catch up. At least with such a busy scene around her, with lecturers demanding their share of attention, she had had to keep her private thoughts in control.

Abruptly, she stopped dead, aghast. Han was leaning against a fence, scrutinising every group of students emerging. His glance passing over one lot came to rest on her, and he straightened. Walking across to her, he said, 'Good afternoon, Miss Bellamy. Your aunt asked me to deliver a parcel to you. It is in the car. Would you care to come over for it?'

Making herself act naturally, astounded at him having the knowledge as to where she was—without the shock of his addressing her by her real name—Christina made herself smile as she answered, 'Hello, Han. Yes, of course,' then with a, 'See you tomorrow,' and a wave of the hand, she turned away from the other girls.

She walked with Han, expecting that more than one gaze was following her with quite some curiosity, and was glad it was only the station-wagon waiting at the kerb. If it had been the Jaguar, goodness knows what they would have thought.

'I'd like to talk to you, Miss Christina,'—not Miss Bellamy, she noticed, and wondered how he had found her in such a short time, and she wondered also if she should go with him, knowing what she did. But this was Han, so she got in through the door of the car which he was holding for her. 'How did you know where I was, Han? In one day?'

'We've always known who you were, Miss Christina.

171

Mr Ashley called in a firm of private detectives the morning after you arrived. He gave it out that his aunt needed references about you. He had a complete dossier on you—and your stepmother and her husband—by Monday evening. He knew all that when he took you to dinner up in the mountains, but he wanted you to tell him yourself.'

Shattered, Christina shook her head, hating that episode in her life, angry with herself for panicking and acting as she had done. She didn't answer.

Han had driven the car on to the Esplanade. 'I don't know why you left, Miss Christina,' he began. 'But before I talk to you, will you answer one question for me truthfully? If the answer is not what I expect, I will drive you straight home.

'Are you in love with Mr Ashley? I mean really, not having just a crush on a very attractive man whom you met in romantic circumstances.'

So, truthfully, she turned to him and replied with one word, 'Yes.'

A sigh escaped from him, a relaxation of the body. 'Then tell me,' he asked, 'why you ran away.'

She couldn't, of course she couldn't answer that, so she sat silent. The man beside her shifted a little, saying, 'I don't know if Mr Ashley would want you to be told, but as it has a bearing on the way he treated you, and even on his way of thinking on one particular subject, I will have to risk my place with him by telling you what I think you should know.

'Our village in Vietnam was overrun. Our two families, Su-lin's and mine, were intermingled, and all that was left of us when it was all over, was Su-lin, her elder sister and little brother, I and my two little brothers. And that was only because we were out in the fields working when it happened. There was nothing left . . . nothing, so we began a trek to the city. Eventually we came up with a convoy of Australians, and one big Sergeant called Jackson gave us a lift. They made a great to-do about the three small boys and Su-Lin, but. . . .' Han gave an ironical smile, 'I expect it was Mai-Ling who got us that lift.'

'Mai-Ling?' queried Christina.

'She was Su-Lin's elder sister, and even at sixteen her beauty caught at you. That was when I began to call Mr Carlton Mr Ashley. It was a name I had never heard before, not like Smith or Brown, and I thought it was his surname. Even when I got to know him better and he told me to drop the Mister, I couldn't. I was only seventeen and he was providing for all of us. Well, I got a job working at a restaurant, and with what food I could scrounge and my tiny wages, I managed to keep the six of us going, even if we were hungry sometimes. Then . . . then Mai-Ling went to live with an American doctor.' Han's voice stopped for a moment, and suddenly Christina was aware, without knowing how, that that face in the photo was of Mai-Ling, not Su-Lin, but she kept silent, and looked as Han was doing—probably with his thoughts flowing back to other years—out over the restless, ever-moving azure waters, on this beautiful peaceful scene before them.

'Then one day,' Han had started again, 'I met Mr Ashley again, with some other Australian soldiers. He still did not look well at all. I stopped to thank Sergeant Jackson for the lift. Mr Ashley asked me, only idly, if it would be possible to get a flat in Saigon. Only a small one, but it had to be self-contained so he could be on his own sometime.

'I laughed! I might have been able to. I knew Saigon by now, going everywhere to find jobs, but Australians were not noted for having a great deal of money. Anything like he wanted would most likely have been taken by the Americans. I told him I possibly could, but he would not be able to afford it. He raised that eyebrow—you know the way he does,' yes, Christina did know, 'and said. "Find me one, Han. Let me worry about the money." '

'So I found a place. He was delighted with it, taking me to a bank to arrange about its upkeep. And, unimaginably for us, there was a shed belonging to it, so we all moved in. Allowed to or not, he left the hospital, going back only every day for treatment. The new arrangement must have suited him, for his colour and his wound began to improve. He returned to his unit ... and Mai-Ling came back to us.

'Then one day he arrived unexpectedly for hospital checks ... and Mai-Ling fell in love with him. You know, don't you, that characteristic charm that is a part of him? Well, they lived together for over a year, and it was the happiest time any of us had ever spent. Of course, Mr Ashley was only there sometimes when on leave, and they were the times when he began to speak our language; always with Mai-Ling, often with me.

'His tour of duty was almost up when Mai-Ling had her photo taken for him. She found a silver frame and made him promise to buy it for her. On the way to do so he was caught up with Army commitments, and decided the frame could wait until the next day.

'However, when we got home, nothing would do for Mai-Ling except to go for it herself. Pushing the half-prepared dinner aside, she got money from Mr Ashley, and went off. We followed, and I remember Mr Ashley was laughing. Then, triumphantly waving the completed photo, she was rushing to meet us when ... when a terrorist bomb went off. Mai-Ling was killed. During the aftermath Mr Ashley hardly spoke, and then only to say it was his fault, that if he had gone himself to get it, Mai-Ling would still be alive. It wasn't his fault. Such an incident could have happened at any time, and underneath it all he knew it, but there it was. People say what he said, about car accidents these days—if only I had not waited for that phone call ... if only we had started when we intended to ... if only.... But accidents belong to fate. I tried, so did the eleven-year-old Su-Lin, to impress upon him how happy he had made Mai-Ling. He was not . . . he had not been in love with her, but he had petted her, indulged her . . . and looked after her.

'He would not live in the flat again. He arranged for an orphanage to take the children, and I went with him back to his unit. Now,' Han's tone abruptly changed, 'that brings me to you. Mr Ashley told me after I had returned from doctoring your leg, "I thought I had killed another young girl, Han. When I saw who it was lying beneath the bumper of the Jaguar, I thought I had killed her . . . another young girl." I got so angry with him for saying such a wrong thing, I almost shouted in return—but about you he has a superstition; a superstition that what happened in Saigon could be repeated if the circumstances were similar.

'He said that when he saw you that first morning confronting his uncle like someone at bay, a determination that no one was going to hurt you overcame him. So after you arrived home from dinner that night and you more than met him halfway when he began to make love to you, he decided he was not going to let you go . . . so marriage was the only alternative.'

'Marriage?' Christina was so startled, the word came out in almost a yelp.

'Yes, he arranged for a special licence on those days he was away in Brisbane, to be married this Saturday. He was going to take you to his aunt's last night, because he did not want you in the penthouse for five whole days, available. . . .

'And now, Miss Christina,' finished Han, 'you owe me an explanation.'

'I thought the girl in the photo was Su-Lin.' She didn't look at Han, and added in a small voice, 'The name was half cut off and I thought Ashley was . . . might be in love with her. . . .'

'In love with Su-Lin?' Astonishment coloured the few words, and then Han started to laugh. He didn't stop, and Christina, who didn't feel like laughing, glared at him.

'Look, I am sorry ... but Mr Ashley hardly knows Su-Lin. He is certainly not in love with her. He is with you!' Flatly, the last words came.

Christina made as if to rise, but his fingers on her arm prevented her. 'Where are you going, Miss Christina?' he asked.

'Why, to him, of course.' She sounded surprised.

'It's not going to be as easy as that, I am afraid. He made no effort to find you. He crumpled your note and threw it away after it was read and stated, "That's that", then began to make preparations for going to America for some cup race.'

'But if I tell him ... if I tell him I thought he was in love with someone else; that anything else about him wouldn't matter ... but for him to be in love with someone else, that's different. . . .' she began.

'He would want to know how you had got such an idea—if he listened to you at all. And I can imagine his reaction to what you did think. . . . No, you must not tell him that,' said Han. 'Also, you have actually got to get in to see him, and there is no way of doing that except with his key—or mine.'

'I could use yours, Han.'

'You could! But if I let you in and he is so furious at what you have done, he would walk past you and leave. I know Mr Ashley. I have seen him in a temper. I would lose too, because he would not take me back. I would chance that if I thought. . . . I only want happiness for him.'

Christina rose, and this time it was with purpose. She said, 'I'm going—we'll think of something. Start the car, Han.'

But standing beside him in the foyer as he unlocked the door to the penthouse, she felt literally sick. It was all right saying they would think of something, but facing Ashley, when he didn't want her there, was another matter. They looked at one another as he swung open the door, then Christina said, 'Lend me your handkerchief, Han, if you have such a thing.'

Astonished, he put a hand to a jacket pocket and pulled out a pristine fold of linen. Flicking it crosswise, Christina tied it round her wounded leg, then taking a deep breath she stepped through, Han closing the door behind her.

Inside there was only silence; the place was softly lighted, but felt empty. Christina walked across the lovely room, turned the corner, then down past her own old quarters, to stand before Ashley's door. Before giving herself time to think, she raised her hand and knocked. Only silence. She knocked again, this time louder.

'Go away, Han!' The voice replying didn't sound angry, didn't sound anything else except for its owner giving an order. She turned the handle and went inside. The man must have felt an alien presence, or heard the door open. He glanced up, and pushed aside a small swivel table on which were piles of papers, with more of them strewn over the side of the bed nearest him. He didn't rise. He put down the pen, and demanded, 'What are you doing here?'

She walked a few steps down the room, and while not aware of saying it, blurted out, 'I came for Han's puffer.'

At that, he did rise, and so did an eyebrow. 'I understood you were in a position to be able to consult a doctor if you felt in need of medical aid.'

At least, she told herself, he hasn't walked past me, and she said as quickly as she could, 'Yes . . . no . . . I mean. . . .' then thought, I can't tell lies. If he won't listen to me, he won't. She bent down to undo the knot of the handkerchief and found the tightened linen wouldn't undo. 'If this was a film or a story it would have parted with a flick,' she spoke defiantly, and pushed it down where it hung sloppily about an ankle.

'Please, Ashley,' she said then, 'will you listen to me for just five minutes, and then I'll walk out of here. Just five minutes!'

'Why? Haven't you been able to find someone among your own friends, your own generation, yet?' Her very words in that letter.

'Oh, don't be stupid, Ashley!' And not even caring that she had spoken thus, she added, 'You know your own attraction—your charisma, if you will have it so. You've had your ... mistresses, your affairs, the countless girls—like Alicia, for instance—who would be wildly delirious at a come-on gesture from you. And ... and after being made love to by you, can you imagine me wanting any other man? When I thought being with you was all over, trying to fill my life with whatever I could was all I thought of—and that didn't include men.'

'You did mention something about five minutes.' A glance was thrown at a wrist watch.

'Yes,' she replied, thinking miserably that he would hear her out and then wait for her to leave. 'Yes,' she said again, 'Han told me not to tell you why I left. He said you'd be so furiously angry at what I'd thought that you would either throw me out or leave yourself. But ... but it *is* what I thought, so you must judge for yourself. When you brought me home on Sunday, I shampooed my hair, and then. . . .'

'Again?' the one word interrupted her.

She glanced at him, a frown beneath her smooth brows at his interjection. 'What do you mean by "again"?'

'I mean that you always seem to be shampooing your hair. I smell it freshly done every time I come near you.' Ashley still wasn't looking at her with any friendliness, and she wondered why he had mentioned such a thing at this time.

She shook her head, and now she wasn't watching him, so she missed a flicker in that impersonal gaze fixed upon her; she was speaking, trying to make her words coherent. 'Then I decided to write a letter and went to ask Han. . . .' She told him the story through to the finish, then stood with her head bowed. He had heard her out in silence. He said now:

'But you've known all along that I haven't—how would you express it?—led a celibate life. And this incredible situation that you describe would have been in my past.'

'Oh,' disdainfully she made a throwaway gesture. 'Of course I realised that. And it would have been the height of impertinence for me to cavil at anything you might have done previously. But I thought . . . Ashley, I thought you must have been in love with her *now* . . . that you couldn't make love to me because you were thinking of her. That was the impediment—for you to be in love with someone now. And you didn't . . . you didn't ever make love to me.'

'No, I didn't, did I? Well, maybe that can be remedied now.' Incredibly, that slur was back in his voice, and he was walking towards her. But he still had that hard, that impersonal look, on his countenance, and she didn't want him to make love to her looking like that. She threw out a restraining hand.

'No? Don't you want that, Christina? I thought that was what this scene was all about?'

She had breathed again at the use of her name, but now she gazed at him critically. She said, 'You don't look as if you want to make love. You look detached . . . impersonal . . . and strange.'

'That's probably because I've been drinking; it will wear off!'

It was said so carelessly, that it was a moment before the import of his words penetrated, then her gaze went searching. His skin *did* have a pallor she had never noticed before; his hair was unruly, all over the place, the yellow gold showing up the citrine streaks more vividly—but his eyes were still the same.

'You haven't been drinking,' she told him positively, 'or at least, not excessively.'

An eyebrow went up and he came closer, and again she put out a restraining hand. 'Please—no, Ashley. So much has happened, I don't know where I am. And I want to tell you how truly sorry I am about Mai-Ling. She must have been very lovely.'

She heard his breath go out in a long sigh; he said, 'Yes, you are, aren't you, Christina? Thank you.' She was swept up in his arms and carried to the bed. Half supporting her with one arm, Ashley swept the papers away to fall where they would. He swung her legs up and with one arm cradling her, they lay together, body to body.

'First things first, though,' that slurred voice was saying, and leaning up on an elbow he reached down to unfasten her sandals which she heard drop to the carpet with a soft thump, then he eased off the handkerchief. Christina saw his bent head below her as he leant down to examine her leg, and only just stopped her hand from reaching out to smooth back the dishevelled, glinting hair. His fingers explored both sides of the groove, then he was back beside her.

'Yes, it is improving . . . and now to more important things. Open your eyes, Christina.' But she shook her head, then felt his lips come down on the corner of hers, rest there for a fleeting second, and then he was kissing her, deeply, achingly . . . like a man coming upon water after emerging from a desert. He acted as such a man might do, too, deliberately limiting himself, for when she arched towards him his lips lifted, his head came up.

'No, Christina,' he said, and then, after a waiting second, 'Did my precious tale-bearing Han tell you any other of my secrets?'

'How do you expect me to concentrate on what you're saying when you're doing that?' she asked in almost a gasp. He was running his finger-tips from temple to throat, to breast, and then down along hips to rest there. . . . A shiver passed through her.

'I told you I'd been drinking; that allows a man a little leeway. *Did* he tell you about any other arrangements I might have made?' His hand was still there, but it was moving. Christina put out the arm that was not trapped beneath him to clasp and hold it, and said, 'Yes, he did. He told me you'd been arranging a wedding, but don't think that had anything to do with my coming back. I didn't care before, I don't now!'

'In that case, my love, I'm sure we can settle for a relationship which doesn't take into account the legal trimmings; especially at this precise moment.' His head came down, his lips following where his fingers had blazed the trail. However, these caresses stopped at the neckline of her dress. 'It's gratifying to realise that I'm being given carte-blanche without any of the responsibilities, and that that state of affairs doesn't worry you.' His hand trailed back, hesitating at her breast, then moved up on to her throat.

'I didn't say it didn't worry me!' her words came breathlessly. 'Of course I'd like orange-blossom and organ music, and the attendant extras that go with them, when I was given to you, but ... with you, Ashley, I'll take anything I'm offered.'

She felt, rather than heard, the form beside her shake with laughter. 'Okay, we won't dispense with all that, but how am I to keep my hands off you for five whole days ... and so much more to the point, for five whole nights? So ... you'll go to my Aunt Beth's for that time.'

'I won't, Ashley.'

The definite statement brought him up on an elbow, looming over her. She said again, taking note of the expression on his face, 'I won't. I'm not going to your aunt's. I'd hate it!'

His voice had lost its slur and any laughter it might have possessed as he replied, 'I'm afraid, Christina, that hating it is going to be too bad for you, because I can't have you around here for five days. I've taken all I can take in that direction, so. . . .'

'You go to your aunt's, then!' Even as she said it, Christina's hand flew to her mouth to prevent the words emerging.

However, Ashley only laughed, and looking down, he moved his hand low against her back, bringing her body to his. 'To use your own words, Christina,' he said, 'I'm not going, I'd hate it.' His arms tightened and she felt his closeness down the whole length of her. Collapsing against him, remembering other times when she had been held so, she shut her eyes, allowing herself to drift, waiting. . . .

She *was* kissed; once only, with a desire that wasn't allowed to get out of hand. And responding as she had always done to the touch of his lips, his caresses, she was aware immediately when Ashley pulled himself free. He looked deep into her eyes as they came open, and dredged up from somewhere a grin as he saw her shake her head. He lifted her with two hands about her waist, on to the other side of the bed, on to the other pillows, then stretched back, both hands behind his head, saying, 'Doesn't that little episode make you understand, Christina? You being here with me just wouldn't work.'

'You could take me back to my motel. I have a room booked there which I expect you know about too.'

'I did know. And you're not going back there.'

'It's only for five days, you said so yourself, and I was perfectly all right there last night.'

'So you were, but there was also a very large detective stationed outside it . . . to make sure you were.'

'Oh!' Christina was abruptly sitting up cross-legged upon the bed, in her turn looking down at him as he lay there so placidly. 'What sort of a detective, and how in the hell did he get outside *my* room?' Indignation ran through the words.

'He was a private detective, and he was there because I gave his boss orders for it.'

'You knew all along where I was!' It was an accusation that she threw at him.

'Of course, and I always intended you to be married on Saturday. I was only giving myself time to discover why you ran away. I will tell you this, however—that never in my wildest imaginings would I have guessed what you did come up with.'

'I was entitled to come up with it, given the evidence. . . .' Christina stopped speaking, furious. Ashley was laughing just as Han had done. She would have loved to hit him, hard. She said instead, 'If your own company amuses you so much, I may as well go!'

A hand flew out to grip a wrist as she made to slip off her side of the bed. 'You're going nowhere—except to your own room along the hall, and we'll have to draw up battle-lines—and keep to them. But first, I'd better go and put Han out of his misery, and advise him that he only knows ninety-nine per cent of what I feel and do—not a hundred per cent. Also, I suddenly find myself starving. Are you hungry?'

She hadn't even thought about it. She did say, 'I don't know about starving, I would like a bath, though. I've been in these clothes all day, working hard.' She glanced across at him and said softly, 'I do love you, Ashley.'

'I know!' he answered, and again she could have hit him. He laughed openly, then swung off the bed. 'Come along, I'll escort you.' He left her at her door, then went along to the entrance, calling back over his shoulder, 'Don't you damn well dare wash your hair! I expect Han to have a decent meal on the table for us in fifteen minutes.'

Anxiously Christina watched Sally put the finishing touches to the tiny flyaway veil that sat on the back cascade of curls, but let the side ones fall free. 'Does it look okay?' she asked.

'If you ask me that again, Elizabeth, I'm going to go

straight back to Sydney ... or, if I thought I had a chance, try to snaffle that husband-to-be of yours! Of course it looks okay, and just as certainly, you look lovely. Heavens, that dress is perfect! You were clever to choose that style.'

'Yes,' said Christina, and didn't enlarge on the subject. She smoothed down the chiffon over the apricot silk and thought that in ten minutes or so she would be married to Ashley. At least the five days had flown, but she had barely seen him. He had phoned Sydney and got Sally up on the nearest plane. He had gone to see Marion, putting on all his considerable charm to smooth over Christina's not being married from home; suggesting that Marion go with her stepdaughter to help buy her trousseau. She had, and she had certainly done it with enthusiasm.

There came Han's tap on the door; his voice telling her that Mr Blythe had arrived. Christina returned his encouraging smile happily, then turned a more nervous one on Ashley's uncle. Then with a rustle of silk, with Sally beside her, she placed her hand lightly on the arm being held out to her, and departed.

She remembered the service; she remembered glancing at Ashley as he placed the ring on her finger. But everything else began to gather a haze-like quality. The last five days had been too rushed; there had been too much to do. Then, suddenly, the reception in the ballroom that Aunt Beth and Ashley's two female cousins had decorated so beautifully was over, and she was changing her wedding dress for the exquisite Italian-knit going-away suit. Mrs Blythe and Marion were fussing around, and Sally was saying, more than a little seriously, even if it was with a smile, 'Don't you dare forget to throw your boquet in my direction, Elizabeth, or I'll never speak to you again!'

She didn't forget. And now they were moving down the driveway in the Jaguar. Christina sat beside Ashley with a hollow feeling under her diaphragm, and wished now that she had eaten from the piled plate Ashley's best man had brought her. She hadn't been able to. She also wondered where they were going. Not, she believed, to Singapore which had somehow got about.

Through the centre of Surfers Paradise, which was beginning to come alive, with brilliant neons flashing, crowds spilling over the footpaths, until the car swished down the familiar ramp to home.

'Tired, my love?' asked her new husband, as he handed her out, and grinned as she only shook her head. Inside, she hesitated, wondering if they did have a plane to catch, but Ashley took her arm and walked down to his own room.

'Well, Mrs Carlton,' he said, 'I don't know about you, but I don't feel like traipsing all over the place when I have a perfectly good accommodation here. Disappointed, Christina?'

'Are we staying here, Ashley?' she asked, and at his nod, threw herself into his arm. 'Oh, I'm glad! Everything has been so hectic. All I want to do is get into any old dress and sit.'

'*All* you want to do, my love?' Ashley's eyebrows had climbed, and Christina felt the blush that ran up to colour her cheeks. 'Right, then, I'll leave you this room, I'll take yours for the moment—but surely not just any old dress? Don't tell me that with all that shopping you didn't buy anything to sleep in! Aunt Beth must be slipping.'

The colour deepened in Christina's face, but she only gave a gurgle of laughter. 'Oh yes, I have something, but I had no intention of wearing it. However. . . . And it wasn't your Aunt Beth, it was Marion. The sheerest of the sheer, and as it was a wedding present, I had to accept it.'

Ashley laughed, saying, 'Don't be long, I'm going to raid the kitchen.'

Snicking the locks of her case open, Christina rummaged round and found the négligé set. She stood, hesitating, then slipping out of the suit, bra and pants, she flipped the nightdress over her head. 'Heavens!' she muttered, and pulled the négligé over it. Shrugging, she unpinned the upswept curls, brushing her hair briskly into its usual style. It didn't fall exactly as it normally did, but Christina was quite satisfied with the extra bounce it showed. Bare feet into scuffs, she went out to meet whatever destiny had in store for her. Ashley wasn't dressed up. All he had on was the well-worn maroon towelling robe.

As she came through the doorway, a wolf whistle wafted across to her. He laughed as she glared at him, and waved her to a chair. 'I didn't eat at that frenzied reception. I bet you didn't either, from what I saw. Just look what I found!'

'Surely in Han's domain, what else would you expect?' she reminded him dryly, and as she passed him, she was pulled back to lean against him, his hands coming round to clasp together at her waist. His head came down, and lips rested on the nape of her neck. He didn't speak, and Christina was unable to. With a sigh he released her, and she sat down abruptly on the chair.

She ate a little; she spoke a little too, but mostly she sat watching Ashley, even now unable to believe that she did indeed belong to him. That now he wouldn't kiss her and then escort her to her room. At one point he glanced up from what he was doing and saw that look. He stopped speaking abruptly, pushed back his chair from the table and reached out a hand.

'Leave it,' he told her harshly, as she made to clear the dishes, and holding a hand, he drew her down the long room. But in his quarters, with the door closed behind them, it was Christina who put out a hand, who, almost stammering, said, 'Ashley, I mightn't ... I mean, you've been around so much. I do love you, but. . . .'

Interrupting her suddenly, by eyes glinting, brimming over with laughter, he said, 'Are you by any chance,

Christina, a young bride on her wedding night, trying to apologise for being a virgin?'

'I hate you!' she told him, and swung away, but was caught and swept up, and carried to the bed. He said, 'We don't want these, and flicked switches on the console by the bed. The chandelier lights went out. 'Or this,' he added, and off went the bedside one. He didn't flick a switch that would operate the curtains over the huge curved windows, but she was sure he would have one for that too.

In the illumination coming in through them, he leaned over her, imprisoning her with an arm outstretched on either side. He said, and the slur had gone from a voice turned serious, 'It will be all right, Christina, I promise you!'

And beside her, outstretched on the bed, his fingers encountered the fragile chiffon. 'We don't want this,' he remarked, 'it impedes me,' and Marion's wedding present was discarded. One arm went beneath, bringing her body to meet his with no reserve at all now. There was no reserve, either, when his lips took possession, sending their demands to every nerve-end.

So too, his hands, finding no impediment, stroked the satin smoothness of her skin, making her heartbeats jump, her breath come gaspingly. All her previous encounters with him had not prepared her for this uninhibited love making, this force of passion and desire being poured out upon her, this unleashed power that almost frightened her. Then the demand, the aching need, changed to slow heartbreaking caresses that washed away all thought, everything but Ashley holding her; and she heard his voice, slurred with emotion, saying softly in the half-darkness, 'Just relax, my love, and come with me. This time we're going travelling together, where delight and rejoicing await us at journey's end.'

 *Harlequin Romance*

Coming Next Month

Available in May wherever paperback books are sold, or through Harlequin Reader Service.

In the U.S.
P.O. Box 1397
Buffalo, N.Y.
14240-1397

In Canada
P.O. Box 2800, Postal Station A
5170 Yonge Street
Willowdale, Ontario M2N 6J3

WORLDWIDE LIBRARY IS YOUR TICKET TO ROMANCE, ADVENTURE AND EXCITEMENT

Experience it all in these big, bold Bestsellers— Yours exclusively from WORLDWIDE LIBRARY WHILE QUANTITIES LAST

To receive these Bestsellers, complete the order form, detach and send together with your check or money order (include 75¢ postage and handling), payable to WORLDWIDE LIBRARY, to:

In the U.S.
WORLDWIDE LIBRARY
901 Fuhrmann Blvd.
Buffalo, N.Y. 14269

In Canada
WORLDWIDE LIBRARY
P.O. Box 2800, 5170 Yonge Street
Postal Station A, Willowdale, Ontario
M2N 6J3

Quant.	Title	Price
	WILD CONCERTO, Anne Mather	$2.95
	A VIOLATION, Charlotte Lamb	$3.50
	SECRETS, Sheila Holland	$3.50
	SWEET MEMORIES, LaVyrle Spencer	$3.50
	FLORA, Anne Weale	$3.50
	SUMMER'S AWAKENING, Anne Weale	$3.50
	FINGER PRINTS, Barbara Delinsky	$3.50
	DREAMWEAVER, Felicia Gallant/Rebecca Flanders	$3.50
	EYE OF THE STORM, Maura Seger	$3.50
	HIDDEN IN THE FLAME, Anne Mather	$3.50
	ECHO OF THUNDER, Maura Seger	$3.95
	DREAM OF DARKNESS, Jocelyn Haley	$3.95

	YOUR ORDER TOTAL	$_____
	New York and Arizona residents add appropriate sales tax	$_____
	Postage and Handling	$___.75
	I enclose	$_____

NAME _____

ADDRESS _____ APT.# _____

CITY _____

STATE/PROV. _____ ZIP/POSTAL CODE _____
WW-1-3

No one Can Resist . . .

HARLEQUIN REGENCY ROMANCES

Regency romances take you back to a time when men fought for their ladies' honor and passions—a time when heroines had to choose between love and duty . . . with love always the winner!

Enjoy these three authentic novels of love and romance set in one of the most colorful periods of England's history.

Lady Alicia's Secret by Rachel Cosgrove Payes

She had to keep her true identity hidden—at least until she was convinced of his love!

Deception So Agreeable by Mary Butler

She reacted with outrage to his false proposal of marriage, then nearly regretted her decision.

The Country Gentleman by Dinah Dean

She refused to believe the rumors about him—certainly until they could be confirmed or denied!

Everyone Loves . . .

HARLEQUIN GOTHIC ROMANCES

A young woman lured to an isolated estate far from help and civilization . . . a man, lonely, tortured by a centuries' old commitment . . . and a sinister force threatening them both and their newfound love . . .

Read these three superb novels of romance and suspense . . . as timeless as love and as filled with the unexpected as tomorrow!

Return To Shadow Creek by Helen B. Hicks

She returned to the place of her birth—only to discover a sinister plot lurking in wait for her. . . .

Shadows Over Briarcliff by Marilyn Ross

Her visit vividly brought back the unhappy past—and with it an unknown evil presence. . . .

The Blue House by Dolores Holliday

She had no control over the evil forces that were driving her to the brink of madness. . . .

Take
4 novels
and a
surprise gift
FREE